Leave the Lamp On...

Sue McCullough

RoseDog Books
PITTSBURGH, PENNSYLVANIA 15238

The contents of this work including, but not limited to, the accuracy of events, people, and places depicted; opinions expressed; permission to use previously published materials included; and any advice given or actions advocated are solely the responsibility of the author, who assumes all liability for said work and indemnifies the publisher against any claims stemming from publication of the work.

All Rights Reserved
Copyright © 2021 by Sue McCullough

No part of this book may be reproduced or transmitted, downloaded, distributed, reverse engineered, or stored in or introduced into any information storage and retrieval system, in any form or by any means, including photocopying and recording, whether electronic or mechanical, now known or hereinafter invented without permission in writing from the publisher.

RoseDog Books
585 Alpha Drive
Suite 103
Pittsburgh, PA 15238
Visit our website at www.rosedogbookstore.com

ISBN: 978-1-6491-3050-1
eISBN: 978-1-6491-3043-3

Introduction

This is a work of historical fiction built on hand-me-down family tales, childhood memories, an over active imagination and a little bit of actual history. If you're a true history buff, you'll notice that I've played rather fast and loose with some of the battles, flow of dates and geography. Much like everything else in life, some are real, others are pure fiction. The central family and supporting characters were real relatives of my Dad's or other folks who were in-laws and friends. Actual names have been used for some of them. Other characters bear the names of real people but they've been borrowed from situations and circumstances that were entirely fabricated. Some people and their names are completely made up.

As I already said, much of this saga is a figment of my imagination but parts are built on truths as told by long deceased relatives. It's up to you, the reader, to figure out what part is true and what part is make believe.

"Memory is a complicated thing, a relative to truth, but not its twin."

- Barbara Kingsolver

DEDICATION

This book is dedicated to the memories of Carl Clarence (Bill) Jones and Vada Viola Jones Parks

FOR VADA, because she was the only one of the Jones children who grew up knowing that their Daddy did try to come back to the family. She knew he tried to see them and to be part of their lives. Vada knew Emily rejected him and denied him time with them.

Vada spent all of her adult life trying to find her Daddy. When she was a young married woman, she tried to find where he was living. Then, as the years went by, she thought that if she could just learn where he was buried, she could put an end to the mystery. She even hired investigators but he was never found.

FOR BILL, my Daddy, because he was the child who bore the burden of standing in the gap left by his missing dad. Bill never really knew anything about life with a father in the house. As an adult, he worked hard to be not just a good father but a good daddy as well. He did his best to make sure his own children had everything they needed. Maybe not everything they wanted but all that they needed. He also made sure his boys knew how to work for what they wanted. But he did tend to spoil his only daughter.

Bill was social and always up for a joke. To Bill, the worst sin a man could commit was failing to take care of his family. Bill spent his whole life never knowing that his own Daddy *did* try to take care of his kids.

THE JONES FAMILY

Charlie Clarence Jones	MARRIED	Martha Emily Pilgrim DeHart
1881/1917	4/8/1905	1883/1953

Clarence and Emily had:

Vada Viola Jones (Fred Parks): 1905/2001

Lloyd Lafayette Jones: 1908/1911

Carl Clarence (Bill) Jones: 1910/1969

Julia May Jones (Ebenezer Adair): 1914/1993

Daughters of Emily and Homer Pilgrim

Myrtis Pilgrim (Rossi): 1901

Virgil Pilgrim (Keller): 1902

Leave the Lamp On...

August, 1915 – Van Zandt County, Texas

Topping a small rise, Martha Emily could see the porch steps, right where her horses and wagon *had been*. Even though it was a scorching August afternoon in East Texas, Emily felt a chill slither down her back under her long, beige cotton dress. She passed baby Julia May to Myrtis and told Virgie to keep an eye on Bill; then she broke into an out and out sprint, calling out "Clarence?" She cleared the steps and crossed the wooden porch into the front room. Louder now, "Clarence, Charlie Clarence, Charlie Clarence Jones … You better answer me!"

Crossing into the front room, she was surprised to see the furniture set inside and boxes stacked randomly, every which way in any open spot on the worn, bare plank floor. Going through the kitchen to the back door, Emily looked toward the small barn, calling out even louder still "Clarence?" No sign of the wagon or the horses.

Silence rang in her ears. She knew he was gone.

A mere 5'5" tall with coal black hair, blue eyes and a cleft chin, handsome Charlie Clarence Jones was restless, always looking for some ill-defined better way to live his life. In 1912, shortly after their baby son Lloyd died of meningitis, Clarence moved the family from Brownsboro, to Eustace, Texas about 15 miles away. As tenant farmers, they worked there for a couple of seasons then in 1915 when his only surviving son, Carl Clarence (Bill) was five, they moved again. This time, he moved the family to Larue. Larue could barely be called a town back then – or now – it was mostly a wide spot where two dirt roads crossed… just east of US Highway 175. At least, the roads are black topped now. Clarence was 34 years old and rarely asked his wife for her thoughts or opinions about anything.

May 8, 1905 at age 24, Clarence had impulsively married Martha Emily DeHart Pilgrim. At that time, Clarence had been boarding with the Sewell family in Northeast

Texas for six years. The Sewell's were tenant farmers with a passel of children. This may have been where Clarence developed his distaste for multiple kids as he'd grown up an only child in the house with an old maid school teacher. Grown up at least until he left home the day he turned 18 years old. We can only speculate about the attraction to Emily DeHart. She was quiet, completely at ease with long droughts of no conversation. And, for that matter, we have no way of knowing what drew Emily to Clarence, other than finding a home and a means of feeding her two young girls.

Emily was a 22 year old widow with two daughters, Myrtis and Virgie. Virgie was actually named Virgil George but was called "Dump" by all who knew her long into adulthood and most of her life. Emily had already buried her first husband, Homer Pilgrim in 1902 just before Virgie was born. By 1915, Emily and Clarence had added four more children, Vada Viola (1906), Lloyd Lafayette, known as Bud (1908) then in 1910, Carl Clarence, who went by Bill. Lloyd died of spinal meningitis in 1911 when the family lived in Eustace. Then in 1914 along came the last of the Jones babies, Julia May. So when Clarence decided it was time to move yet again, they were carrying quite a load even before adding furniture, clothing and the general bits and pieces of daily life.

With the entire household packed onto the wagon, Emily began loading children into any crevice she could find. The three older girls, Dump, Myrt and Vada, were none too happy with this arrangement but five year old Bill thought it was great fun to be strapped to the dining table on the back of the wagon. Leaving the Eustace farm for the last time, Clarence didn't give the place a backward glance. But Emily swallowed burning tears as she cradled a napping Julia May. It wasn't the plain, unpainted ramshackle farmhouse with no running water that she would miss. Nor the tall pines swirling fragrantly in the breeze. She was leaving her memories of healing after the loss of Bud. It was the memory of Bill's first tooth coming in. Then the fall from the front porch that chipped a piece off that first tooth. Her life had been in upheaval for more than ten years. She thought surely it was time for her days to settle down. She even welcomed the thought of routine and maybe a little boredom.

By early-afternoon, the Jones family had reached the new place in Larue, another small, unpainted wood frame house, just the same as all the others they had lived in. The family was met on their own front porch steps by the next door neighbor, a Mrs. Clark. Mrs. Clark insisted that the family come across the bare field for lunch and a rest before the unloading began. Emily hesitated. She was shy around new people but Clarence insisted that they go.

"Just to be polite, Em" whispered Clarence.

So off they went, to a fine, large country meal of fried chicken and gravy, creamed potatoes, green beans, sliced ripe tomatoes, cornbread, sweet tea, pound cake and stilted conversation. Emily thought it odd that Mrs. Clark was home alone, except for a crib baby and a little blue eyed girl about three years old, but had a huge mid-day meal prepared just at the moment the Jones' rolled up. No mention was ever made of the whereabouts of a Mr. Clark. But, food was food and her children were hungry.

After the clink of forks on the plates slowed to a stop, Emily stood up and stretched, ready to get the afternoons chores behind her. As was her manner, she crisply announced "Clarence, let's go get to it." But Clarence just heaved a deep sigh and said,

"Why don't you rest a bit more? You and the kids. I'll go start unloading then y'all come on in an hour or so."

Surprised, Emily retorted, "I don't need any more rest than you do. I'm perfectly able to do my share of the work."

"I know. I know... I know you are, Em. But maybe the kids could use some more time to get to know this new little friend here and you can help Mrs. Clark clear up the dishes."

Emily stared at Clarence, mouth open and jaw working but, for once, she held her tongue and made no return comment.

Mrs. Clark ducked her head but said not a word. Clarence rose from the table, mumbled a "thanks" for the hospitality, gathered his hat from the hook by the rusty screen door, letting it slam as he bolted across the porch and back toward their own new homestead.

"I'm sorry for those cross words in your home, Mrs. Clark. Clarence and I forget our manners sometimes."

"Same as the rest of us," smiled Mrs. Clark. "Don't give it another thought. How about another glass of tea? And, please, I'm just 'Cora' – none of this MRS. Clark business. All right, Emily?"

At last, Emily seemed to relax a little, "It'd be a pleasure. Thank you for the kindness . . . Cora."

So Emily and Cora spent another leisurely hour drinking tea, picking at cornbread crumbs, talking about men, sick babies and hot weather, just getting to know each other. Then, Emily rose again, beginning to stack plates and clear the table. Cora stopped her. "Don't bother yourself with any of that. It'll take me longer to find everything after you help me than if I just do it myself in the first place."

Emily actually laughed, "That's the gospel truth. I better be getting on then before Clarence has everything put away and it takes me a week to find the cook stove."

Emily rounded up her three girls, Myrt, Virgie & Vada, and then scooted Bill down the porch steps. Heading toward an afternoon of unpacking boxes under their mother's critical eye, the girls were not in any hurry. Oldest of the children, Myrtis picked up Julia May, barely a year old but Emily took the baby from her. Settling "Sis" astraddle her tiny waist, and with her free hand, she hiked up the hem of her skirt and struck a trot across the rough field.

Topping a small rise, she could see the porch steps, right where the wagon *had been*. Even though it was a scorching August afternoon, Emily felt a chill slither down her back. She passed Julia May back to Myrtis, told Virgie to watch out for Bill, and then she broke into an all out sprint, calling out "Clarence?" as she cleared the steps and crossed into the front room. "Clarence, Charlie Clarence... You better answer me!"

Inside, she was surprised to see the furniture set in and boxes stacked randomly, every which way in any open spot on the worn plank floor. Going through to the back door, Emily looked toward the small barn, calling out even louder still "Clarence?" No sign of the wagon or the horses.

Silence rang in her ears. She knew he was gone.

As Emily turned back toward the kitchen, nine year old Vada walked toward her mother, holding out an envelope. "I found this on the table. Want me to open it for you?"

"No, I do not. Give it here." Emily tore the envelope open to find a single page note. It read:

> *"Em, I'm sorry but this farming life is not for me. I need to be in a town. The responsibility – all these kids – I can't do it. Somebody is always needing, wanting, whining for something. There's never a quiet moment to breathe. It's just choking me to death. I've tried but it just isn't working out. I'll miss the children ... and you. I'll be in touch through Slick."*

Emily's older brother, Gordon (Slick) DeHart lived just down the road a piece – maybe a short mile - from this new place in Larue. Clarence and Slick were old friends. So, Emily sent Virgie and Myrt down to his place with instructions to tell their stepdaddy to "get on back home for supper."

"Oh" with narrowed eyes and a little half smile, Emily added, "Invite Uncle Gordon and Aunt June, too."

Recognizing that look on their mama's face, the girls took off as fast as they could after Myrtis plopped Julia May down on the dusty, old braided rag rug in the middle of the floor. They sure didn't want Emily to turn her icy anger on them. Julia May played quietly, patting the faded colors on the old rug while Vada tried to keep Bill busy and out from under foot. The children always knew when their mother was upset, so they did their best to avoid any additional aggravations. But, this time, there was not another word out of Emily as she resolutely set about unpacking the first box she saw. Luckily, it was dishes, kitchen utensils and other various housekeeping items.

Less than an hour had passed when Virgie and Myrtis clattered back through the front door with Uncle Gordon and Aunt June hot on their heels.

"What the h-hell is going on?" demanded Slick.

Emily shot back "I thought to ask you that same question, Gordon. Where is Clarence? I know you two must've cooked up some plan to do something stupid."

Gordon, called "Slick" by absolutely everyone except Emily, puffed up, color climbing up his neck like an angry tide, from his khaki shirt collar right up to his curly red hair line. Slick's wife, June, glanced at Emily then back at Slick and back to Emily again. As usual with these sibling disputes, she was caught in the stunned middle. Never quick on his feet, Slick stood staring at Emily with his mouth hanging open.

Emily was a fierce little woman, not a fraction over five feet tall and about three biscuits shy of 100 pounds. She had almost-curly, fine, golden hair that she struggled to pull back into a tight little knot. Her resting expression was one of near hostility with a clamped jaw, pursed lips and narrowed eyes. Slick was scared to death of his baby sister.

After a long silence stretched out that bothered everyone except Emily, June found her tongue, elbowed Slick in the ribs and advised "You better speak up. She'll have knuckle bumps all upside your head here in the next couple of minutes."

In the middle of much throat clearing, Slick stammered out, "M-M-Martha EmEmily, you you know I'd never do anything to h-hurt hurt you . . . or them childern." Slick tended to stutter and stammer when he was nervous . . . and he was nervous a lot. Emily was having none of it.

"Gordon, Clarence did not unload all this furniture and the boxes off that wagon, set it all in this house and get gone in an hour. Not by himself, he didn't. You knew when we'd be getting here. Isn't it convenient that here you are at home – smack dab in the middle of the day. Why aren't you at work anyway?"

Slick took a step back as though he'd been struck in the gut. In the same instant, June sucked in a huge gasp. They exchanged glances but neither spoke. Slick suddenly decided he needed to sit down and re-lace his boots.

Heaving a loud grunt, Clarence wrestled a packed-full dresser off the wagon onto the wood steps leading to the plank board porch. Sweat stung his eyes and dripped off his nose, spotting down the front of his faded chambray shirt. Clarence had never minded hard work but he detested being dirty. Stopping to gain a breath, he jumped like a guilty man when a deep voice close to his ear said, "You're about to bust a gusset there, man."

"Slick, what are you doing here? Thought you'd joined up and would be gone already."

"I d-d-did join up. Went over to Athens this morning and registered. I can leave any time in the next week. Boy, let me tell you. J-J-JuneBug ain't happy. But a man has to stand up for his country. Say, where is my baby Sister and all your young uns? Guess I might as well tell her what's up and let her be mad, too."

Clarence shuffled a bit, as best he could while holding up the end of the dresser, one foot on the ground, the other on the second step. He glanced up at Slick and said, "Why don't you use some of those muscles there, boy? You're gonna need the practice soon enough. Grab that end and help me with this thing."

Slick was a much bigger, beefier man than 5'5" Clarence so with one solid yank, he heaved the dresser the rest of the way up the steps and through the open screen door in one swift motion. Suddenly finding his own arms empty and his body off balance from his feet, Clarence collapsed in a heap right there on the bottom step.

"You big ox, you nearly caused me to break my neck."

"What are you wh-whining about? Dresser's in the house, ain't it?!" Slick replied with his usual grin.

The two men fell to the task, working quickly and quietly in tandem. They'd been friends for more than 20 years so they knew each other's rhythm. Clarence hauled boxes while Slick wrestled furniture, waiting for help only on the wood stove and the bathtub. The house had running water in the kitchen but no indoor bathroom. The three foot long tub was porcelain over cast iron and weighed about half a ton. Clarence had argued to leave it at the old house in Eustace but Emily wouldn't hear of it. She was adamant about having a tub for her girls. And "NO, a galvanized metal trough in the yard will NOT do. Those are for horses, not young ladies." Cussing under every breath, Slick and Clarence wrestled the tub off the wagon, onto the porch then through the living room into the kitchen where it came to rest in a corner close enough to draw water from the sink and then to siphon and drain it out the back door.

Clarence declared, "I hope Emily will be happy now. She won't have to pump well water to fill that blasted thing. I promise you one thing, Slick DeHart. That's the LAST time I'm moving that damn bathtub. I don't care if those girls get dirty enough to grow turnips in their ears."

In pretty short order, the unloading was done so Slick asked Clarence where to begin inside the house. Clarence replied that the inside work would need to wait until Emily got there to direct placement.

"No point in doing it twice. You know we won't get it right."

"You never did say where Emily and the kids are. You didn't go off and forget 'em back in Eustace now did you?"

Married 15 years, Slick and June couldn't have children. June didn't dwell on the matter much. Tall, slim June enjoyed life without the uproar of children since she was raised in the Buckner Baptist orphanage in Dallas County. She didn't know the privacy of a locking bathroom door until she was 19 years old. She loved not having to scuffle for every crumb to eat as much as she loved not having to share Gordon's attention. Well, only with his sister, Emily. But Slick missed what he called "fun fatherhood" after growing up in a noisy household with a set of loving parents in Jacob and Judith DeHart. As much as he loved life with June, he would've loved having 'kiddos' in the house. He doted on Clarence and Emily's kids and was thrilled that they would be living close enough to spoil them a bit; especially his little nephew, Bill.

"What makes you ask such a thing, Slick?" Clarence replied in a defensive tone.

Though Slick and Clarence had been friends since their teen years, long before they became in-laws, Slick never was quite sure how trust worthy Clarence was. He thought Clarence always seemed edgy, like a cat about to pounce on a field mouse. Just waiting for the perfect moment to pull some stunt. It was at those times that Slick would shake his head to rid himself of such doubts and remind himself that Clarence had married his baby sister when she was already widowed with two girls fathered by another man. Shoot, he HAD to be a good guy, didn't he?

"Awhile ago, I asked you where Emily and the kids were. You never did say."

Clarence looked at Slick and said, "Well, if you're writing a book. . . They're at the new neighbors…Cora Clark's house across the south field yonder. She had lunch ready when we got here and just insisted that we come over to eat. Em will be along directly."

"Well. W-Well. Well, h-how convenient for you. Hope the two girls get to be g-g-good friends. Something tells me, they g-gonna be needing each other, you no-no good old d-dawg."

Instead of being angry, Clarence just snorted out a laugh and said, "I ain't done nothing wrong. You're the one who snuck off and enlisted. Shouldn't you be getting on back home before June throws your drawers out onto the front yard? I appreciate the help but I want to get a few more things done before Emily comes in with all the kids – and their endless questions. We'll see y'all later, after supper."

Slick waved, jumped from the porch and took off at a clip down the road toward his own house. June would have iced tea waiting with some peach cobbler. Slick quickened his steps a bit. June loved cooking and was mighty good at it.

Turning back into the front room, Clarence made a bee line to the dresser that had been placed along the back wall of the four room house. A living room, two bedrooms and a kitchen would serve the family of seven. Baby Julia May still slept in a crib in the room with Clarence and Emily. Myrt, Virgie and Vada would share the other bedroom. Bill would have a pallet on the braided rag rug in the living room. Clarence pulled out a clean, starched and folded shirt then shucked the sweaty one, tossing it into the corner behind some boxes. Pulling out the bottom dresser drawer, he rooted around under some quilts and winter things until he found an envelope. Counting the bills inside, he started to take out a few then hesitated, mumbling to himself. He then quickly stuffed all the money inside his shirt. He wished he could take the time to find the box with his shaving mug, razor and hair tonic. But stopping to look for them would be begging for trouble.

Sure he was about to be caught, Clarence was edging close to panic now. So he hurried out the kitchen door, down the back steps, heading toward the barn. Suddenly he stopped in his tracks.

"Dammit to hell and back!" Clarence blurted out loud. Wheeling around, he headed toward the side of the house and on to the front where the emptied wagon still waited. In his haste, he had forgotten that the horses had been left standing in the blazing sun for more than two hours, unfed and unwatered. Now, there was no time to tend to them properly. "Well, maybe they'll forgive me one more time" he thought to himself as he climbed onto the wagon seat, picked up the reins and snapped the team to a trot. Turning toward Slick's place, Clarence blew out a guilty sigh. The bit of remorse he felt passed quickly, though.

Judging by the sun, Clarence figured it was somewhere around 4 o'clock; Too late to get in to Athens to the recruiters office today. Seeing Slick's place just ahead, he slowed a bit then pulled off the road into the side pasture. Following the recently turned dirt rows to minimize his tracks, he crossed to the tree lined, white rock shallow creek that ran along the back of the property. Stopping beneath a tall, leafy oak tree, he jumped down then unhitched the team, leading them over to drink their fill.

Even though he and Slick were friends . . . and June tolerated him . . . Clarence had not shared his plans with Slick. Because, after all, Slick was his wife's brother. Besides, a secret don't keep once a second person has it in their pocket, ready to spend like a silver dollar.

Staying in the shadows of the trees, Clarence worked his way toward the barn, stepping out into the light at the last possible moment then ducking inside to grab up the oat bag. He crept back out then retraced his steps to the creek and his horses.

Now that the team was fed, watered and content, Clarence dipped his hands in the cool water & wiped his face. Cupping them, he took a drink himself. Then, he stretched out in the shade under the wagon to consider the next days' plan. Less than five minutes later, he was snoozing soundly.

Startled by young voices, he sat bolt upright at full attention, cracking his head like a boiled egg on the bottom of the wagon. He could hear Myrtis and Virgie inside, talking excitedly to Slick and June. Though he couldn't make out the words, the tone told him all he needed to know. Slick's angry stutter was crystal clear and he knew he better make tracks as soon as possible, maybe before first light in the morning.

In short order, the front screen door slammed and all four – Myrtis and Virgie followed immediately by Slick and June – took off back down the road toward Emily's. Clarence spent less than five seconds wondering why they went on foot instead getting the buggy from the barn. As soon as they were out of sight, he headed straight in the back door into the kitchen to find a bite to eat. A whole ham sat on the counter, ready to slice. Clarence found a knife and cut a couple of small pieces – nothing big enough to be noticed. Crackers from the jar would be tasty, though a little dry. He spied a fresh peach cobbler on the table that smelled so tempting but it was untouched, obviously meant for later so he didn't dare. Leaving that pie was difficult since Clarence had a terrible sweet tooth. Washing & drying the knife he'd just used then returning it to the drawer, he took his plunder and headed back toward the creek. He ventured across to June's garden, plucking a ripe tomato as a perfect 'go with' for his ham and crackers.

Settling back down in the shade, he ate the ham and crackers. That fresh tomato added enough moisture to be just about perfect. He went to the creek again for a drink then moved the wagon farther back behind the barn before settling down in the shade to wait. In just a few minutes, with a full belly, he was snoozing again.

Shuffling hooves and whinnies quickly brought him back around. He heard Slick whistling inside the barn so he jumped up and quieted the horses. He sure didn't want Slick to discover him lurking in the dusky dark. After what seemed like an eternity, Slick whistled his way out of the barn and back to the house but within just a minute or so, he slammed back into the yard, returning to the barn.

"Thunderation! What's he doing now!?"

But Slick didn't tarry long. In just a couple of minutes, he came back out, stopping in the middle of the yard to glance back toward the creek then going on inside, Clarence heard the latch set on the back door. "Wonder why he latched the screen?"

Keeping still and quiet, Clarence watched a light come on inside the house then, through an open window, he could hear June start the grilling. "Slick, what is Clarence up to? You might as well tell it. Obviously he's up to no good and you know all about it. You're no better than he is! Helping him cook up some ridiculous plan that will, no doubt, break your baby sister's heart! How could you get involved in such nonsense?"

Slick paced and listened for a little while then finally, he spewed out, "Dad Gummit, J-J-June! I don't know why you always th-think I'm helping Clarence with some scheme! You know he's forever dreaming of some way to try to live high on the h-h-hog. Does it look like to you we're l-l-living in the lap of l-l-luxury? Well? Does – D - DOES it!? Why do you think I've signed up in the Army except to help us on down the road? . . . In the future … I ain't leaving you! And it ain't j-j- just for f-fun… Besides that, joining up to serve our Country is what a r-real man, any-any man would do right now."

"Okay, calm down, *Gordon*. It's all right. I know you're planning for us to be together again as soon as the war is over. And it won't be long. I didn't mean anything by those questions. You know I just don't trust Clarence. Never have. Besides if he does something to upset Emily, we'll all have to suffer for it and you know THAT's the gospel truth!"

"Y-y-you're right about Emily making everybody m-m-miserable. I feel bad for those children. They've all b-been through enough already. Now, you and me b-both need to get some s-s-sleep. Tomorrow will be here right on schedule and I'm not looking forward to saying good-bye. In fact, I-I-I don't think I will say it – I'm just gonna get up and go quickly and quietly." Slick then wiggled into a spot under the light weight summer blanket.

June laughed right out loud at that idea. Slick had never done anything 'quietly' in his life – the big ol' lovable oaf. But she said nothing, just settled down under the wash worn blanket next to Slick with a fearful, ragged sigh. Then, just before dozing off, she heard Slick mumble, "Don't call me Gordon." So, June was laughing a little when she finally fell asleep herself.

Slick lay still, eyes wide open until he heard the whiffling long breath that told him June was sound asleep. Then, he continued to lay awake, thinking about what was waiting ahead, in just a few short hours. What WAS Clarence up to? Leaving Emily and those five kiddos alone with nobody to help put food on the table. What would become of them? Then, back to his other worry; would June really wait for him until the war was over?

With those nervous thoughts circling, Slick slipped out of bed and headed to the kitchen where he dipped up two bowls of that delicious peach cobbler than Clarence had spied earlier. Looking across the moonlit backyard toward the barn, Slick caught sight of Clarence slinking down toward the creek, wearing just his long johns. Always ready to pull a prank, Slick quickly eased out the door and hurried into the shadows beside the barn. Once inside, he snatched up Clarence's pants and boots, planning to hide them in the hay. But he heard Clarence swear when he stepped on a rake that had been left on the ground. So, Slick set down the bowls of cobbler on a hay bale then scurried up the short ladder into the loft, flopping down, out of sight if Clarence happened to glance up. But Clarence didn't look up or even notice that his pants were missing. He just stretched out in some fresh hay that he'd spread and was soon snoring, missing the cobbler altogether.

Slick hadn't figured on spending his last night at home in the hayloft so after about a half hour, he stood up to sneak back to the house. The dried, old wood of the loft floor sang out with a mighty screech under Slick's 200 pounds.

Startled awake, Clarence jumped straight up then discovered that his boots and all his meager belongings were missing from the barn. No pants, no boots, no nothing. He was suddenly angry beyond reason. "Dad-Gummit to Hell," he spewed aloud but remembered not to shout.

A choking sound echoed back from the loft just above his head. Clarence paused to listen but then all he heard was the wind rustling up another hot August day. That, and a few roosters practicing to announce the approaching daylight. He took a single step toward the door when his bare foot found a still warm horse patty. Forgetting caution, Clarence let out a stream of oaths that would frizz hair in the local beauty shop; the Curl Up and Dye.

At this, the choking sound returned, but this time it bubbled into a full blown guffaw. Slick dropped down from the loft, tossing Clarence his pants and boots. When Slick could stop laughing, he said "You think you're the quietest thing since sundown. Boy, you're so stupid. June asked me last night, 'How long is Clarence going to slip around the yard and sleep in the barn?' Sounds like a cow stuck in a muddy ditch.' "

Clarence huffed and replied, "Y'all will be happy to know that I'm leaving at first light. I'm going to Athens to join the Army. Somebody has to go along to make sure you get back to June . . . and your baby sister . . . alive and in one piece."

Slick gulped then stammered, "You must b-b-be joking. You ain't doing no-no-no such thing. What about Emily? She might let you come home as long as you get on back this morning. If you don't, she's liable to report you to the po-lice for deserting the family. What about your kids? Who's gonna feed them?"

"Emily won't go to the police. She'll be fine. She'll find somebody else."

Slick stepped back to sit down on a bale of hay, wringing his hands, he said, "If you join up and g-g-go with me, does that mean you ain't planning on-on-on coming back home?"

Chuckling, Clarence answered, "Course I do but that could take a year or maybe more. Can you imagine how mad Em would be if I just showed back up after that long? You know how she mad she gets if I even forget to set the egg basket in the right spot on the kitchen table. And with you gone, too?"

Slick's face relaxed just a bit, "Durn your hide. Actually, I'm a l-l-little glad to be going now. Those Germans can't be half as bad as Emily on the warpath. I brought you a bowl of peach cobbler so I guess it's as a send off treat."

So it was decided. Clarence and Slick would go to Athens together; Slick would head off to boot camp and Clarence would enlist, leaving immediately if that's how it worked. Or, following Slick shortly. Slick went back into the house to give June the news and to gather some road food. Clarence got his kit back together and waited.

Stocked with fried egg sandwiches, cookies and peaches, and with June waving from the back door, Clarence and Slick left before the chickens got up. In Clarence's wagon, they rode in silence nearly all the way to Athens. Clarence was lost in his own thoughts and Slick was worrying about his baby sister. He wasn't concerned about June. She'd been relieved to find out that he and Clarence would be together. He knew June thought he couldn't actually take care of himself on his own. And Slick was about half way afraid she might be right.

Finally Clarence spoke, "It's not likely we'll ship out together, you know. Especially if they know we're sort of related. I've heard they don't like to have kinfolk stationed together to cut down on possible multiple casualties in one family."

"Why'd you have to go-go-go and bring something like that up. You know I d-d-d-don't like to talk about that s-sorta thing. Even if facing Emily is s-s-scarier than anything else, I can't think of-of THAT . . . not right now," worried Slick.

And so, Slick was jumpy for the rest of the ride into Athens.

Clattering into the Athens town square, Clarence headed to the enlistment office. Slick jumped off the wagon seat before they stopped rolling. He grabbed their bags, skimpy though they were, plopped them down on the sidewalk and dropped next to them, and began chewing at his fingernails. Clarence drove on east up Main Street to a livery stable where he could make arrangements for the wagon and team to be taken back to Emily. He made sure to tell the stable boss that Emily is a "little spitfire who knows her own horses so it wouldn't be healthy to try and swap a pair of old nags for that fine team of Roans."

15 minutes later, Clarence strolled on back around the corner to find Slick in the midst of a full blown melt down; staring at the ground, pacing, mumbling aloud to himself and wringing his hands. Stepping in front of Slick, Clarence put his hands up on his shoulders. "Hey, there, boy. You gotta calm down. You're gonna faint dead away." Slick glanced at Clarence as though he were a rank stranger, shook out from under his hands then reversed his path on the sidewalk. Clarence stayed beside him, speaking in soft tones. "Listen, Slick, you're getting all worked up for no reason. You don't have to join. You can go right into that office and tell them you've changed your mind. Something has come up. That your family needs you here. That you've got two farms to run and a passel of abandoned children to feed."

Slick stopped walking and, without looking at Clarence said with no hesitation, "You know once you've signed up, you have to go. There ain't no "Never Mind" about it. It's just that, all of a sudden, I'm kind of worried. Especially now that I know y-y-you don't intend to ever come back. AND that we-we won't be t-t-together."

Clarence responded, with a bit more 'Stern' in his voice than he usually had with Slick. "You need to get that out of your head. I told you that I'm coming back, no matter how mad Emily might be. Besides, you didn't even know that I was joining up until this morning. You made the decision to go to war all on your own without me. Now, come on inside and let's get this registration thing done."

Slick heaved a sigh that would've blown him backwards into the street if he wasn't so hefty. He stuck his chin out, ran his hands through his curly red hair, hitched his pants up and headed toward the recruitment office door where the uniformed young corporal spent his day behind an orderly, clean desk, moving paperwork from one side to the other. The officer was flanked on each side by flags, the 46 starred United States flag on one side and the Lone Star State flag on the other. There were two straight backed, cushionless chairs in the middle of the room, facing the desk. The scrubbed pine floor was not polished but it was so clean, it fairly gleamed. Catching the sun from the big front windows, it gave off a welcoming air. Against the wall at the far end of the square room stood an old wooden library table with two more chairs. Even though it was August in East Texas, the room felt cool.

The young corporal had been watching the nervous red-headed guy out front for the last ten minutes. When he signed the man up yesterday, he wasn't so jittery and jumpy. His actions now didn't match yesterday.

Slick charged right up to the fledgling officer and announced, "Gordon DeHart . . . Reporting for d-duty. But in case you f-f-forgot, mostly I'm known as 'Slick.' And this here is C-Charlie Clarence Jones. He has-has decided to join up and come along with me. To sort of p-protect the fam-family interest, don't you see?"

Clarence groaned and turned back to face the door. Slick heard him and said, "Whaaaat?!?!"

Clarence turned back around to face the officer and said, "I'm here to enlist and do whatever is needed, wherever the country needs me to go. It's true that I *am* Charlie Clarence Jones."

Pulling a stack of papers from the right hand top desk drawer, the young Army man handed them to Clarence, asking "Do you know how to read and write?"

Taken slightly aback, Clarence said, "Well, yes, I certainly do. And, I can do arithmetic pretty well, in case you want to know that, too."

Slick lit up and said, "I don't know about his r-r-reading but he sure can figure – he can build a barn that's perfectly true."

Clarence turned toward Slick and declared, "Please, I can do without your help. Thank you."

Embarrassed, Slick looked down at the worn smooth, wooden floor and started ringing his hands again.

The Corporal told Clarence to have a seat at the table, fill out the paperwork then give it back. Turning to Slick, who he'd kept an eye on during the exchange with Clarence, he said, "Mr. DeHart, did you bring all your paperwork back today." Slick didn't answer, he just continued staring at the floor then over at Clarence then to the front door. Floor, Clarence, Door. Floor, Clarence, Door – over and over.

Corporal loudly cleared his throat, asking again, "MR. DeHART. Did you bring the finished papers back to me?"

No response. Clarence couldn't take it anymore and said, "Slick, he's talking to *you*!"

Slick glanced up at him when he realized that HE was "Mr. DeHart" and replied, "I told you that I go by "Slick" – Mr. DeHart was my daddy."

Corporal had begun to question the signing of this recruit when Slick pulled the rumpled paperwork from the bib of his overalls. When Corporal read over the forms, he discovered that while all the answers were in the correct boxes and technically accurate, there was reason to wonder if 'Slick' would adapt to military life, life in a war zone at that. He seemed awful skittish and dependent on this other guy, Charlie Clarence Jones.

"Are you two gentlemen related?"

Slick stated proudly, "Charlie Clarence here is my brother-in-law, married to my b-baby sister, Martha E-Emily for more'n 10 years now. Let-let me tell you, if he can survive that long with Emily and their five young uns, he can do a fine job over there in the war. He just decided to come along to make sure I'd stay s-s-safe. Safe."

Clarence never looked up from his paperwork during Slick's calm speech. He just clenched his jaw and kept penciling in boxes. Young Corporal recognized the situation for what it was and made up his mind in that moment about what he needed to say to Slick but decided to wait until Clarence gave him the completed forms. He thought Charlie Clarence Jones did seem to have the makings of a good soldier, even if he was a little long in the tooth.

Finished with his task, Clarence stood up from the table and gave the forms back to Corporal who perused them without a word. Corporal pushed back his chair, rising to look at Clarence then, clearing his throat, said, "I think that you will be an asset to the military ranks. However, I've come to believe that Gordon will be of better use to his country by staying here, helping out his sister with her children until you return home."

Clarence looked back at Slick who hadn't moved a muscle. "Slick, did you hear the man? You can head on back home. You don't have to join the Army after all. I'll go for both of us."

There was a long silence in the room. All three men, waiting.

Slick finally spoke, "Well, now. I see. Y'all don't – don't think I'm s-s-s-smart enough to fi-fi-fi... fight in the Army. I'm the one one one who took the first step, coming here on my-my own to j-j-join up. And you-you, Clarence, fol-followed me cause you think-th-th-think it's a way to get shed of your re-responsi-bi-bi-bilities here at home. I know better than 'You-you-you just want to-to p-p-protect me.' You're abandoning Em-Emily and the children!'"

Clarence stepped forward with his hand extended as if to take Slick's arm but he jerked away. This time, Slick wasn't nervous – he was angry. The quiet anger of a person unfamiliar with the feeling. An angry person who could turn dangerous at the drop of the wrong word or move.

Corporal pushed back from his tidy desk, stepping around toward Slick but Clarence motioned him back.

"Slick, you're right. When you decided to join, it gave me the idea of taking this opportunity to start a new life. You know how I hate farming. Been doing it since I was 12. Never been any good at it. There has to be a better way to make a living. A better way to provide for Emily and the kids. Maybe I'll learn in the Army. And Yes, I'll be back. As soon as the war is over, or they get tired of me, whichever. But I *will* be back. I'll make sure Emily knows my plan. Maybe Corporal here is right. You stay here… Let me go in your place… You stay here and help Emily some – as much as she'll let you. Be here for June. Maybe that is the best plan after all….. Don't you think so?"

"I th-think it's the easy-easy way out for you. Y-y-you go off and l-l-eave me here to face Emily. June is a d-d-dear. She under-understands that I was only going to try to build a better future for us and to serve our Country…"

Slick stood silent, simmering. Without another word, he just looked at Clarence then turned to Corporal. "Give me my papers back. I'm not taking any chances on you making a mistake and forgetting to take me off the enlisted roster. Then me end up getting arrested for being a deserter," Slick said without any pause or hesitation.

Corporal replied, "Oh, there won't be any mistakes … but I have to keep the forms. Government property, you know."

Slick tensed up again and repeated, louder this time, "Give me my papers back.

YOU may be government property but I'm not. According to you and C-C-Clarence, my *best buddy* here, I'm not *worthy* of getting shot at for my country."

"Now just a minute there, Mr. DeHart. Nobody said..."

"No, YOU wait a m-minute. You've said plenty. Besides, what you don't say is just as loud as the words you DO use. That goes for you, too, Clarence. You all think I'm slow and couldn't take care of myself but you're wrong. You're both wrong. So far, I've been calm about everything but I'm just about at the end of my rope. Now give me them damn papers before I get mad."

Clarence raised an eyebrow at Corporal but said nothing. Corporal seemed to visibly shrink but he took a deep breath then held the stack of forms out toward Slick who snatched them away. Slick turned toward Clarence and opened his mouth as if to give him what for but instead just shook his head and left the office.

Clarence and Corporal stood in silence, watching Slick stomp around on the sidewalk a couple minutes then jump to the ground and take off at a trot. Then, Clarence let out a long breath and said, "Well, that went better than it might have."

To which Corporal replied, "Oh, shut up. You be back here at noon tomorrow, ready to ship out. Better not have a 'change of heart' now that your kin won't be along with you."

Clarence stepped outside of the enlistment office and looked west. He could still see Slick, but just barely, as he paced that long legged gait toward home. Clarence went back to the livery stable to see if they'd taken the wagon and team back to Emily yet. Ah, his lucky day. The horses were still in the stalls. He retrieved them and headed home himself. Catching up behind Slick, he hollered ahead, "Hey old buddy. Want a ride?"

No response.

"Hey, don't be mad. You should be happy that you don't have to go to war. And, it's not like you didn't try. June will be thrilled."

Slick snapped, "As usual, you think you're so smart. You've used me – again. You've cooked up this whole plan. You knew that if you left E-Emily to join the Army she'd be mad but would get over it since it's for the Cause. You talked about getting killed so I'd get all rattled and probably panic. And either back out or get thrown out. Well, it worked. Now, you get to be the big hero and I get to go home to be the fool - again. You must be real proud. It didn't even occur to you that I was going to try and build a better life for June and me so we could take care of our own children someday - maybe. No, as always, it's all about you, Clarence. All about you."

Unphased by the outburst, Clarence replied, "You want a ride or not?"

"NO."

Clarence slapped the reins and urged the horses up to a trot. "Suit yourself. I leave tomorrow at noon. I'll be back in a year or so, Good Lord willing."

Dark slips in late in the summer but the kids had already finished supper and had been sent off to bed by the time Clarence slowed the horses at the edge of the yard. He sat there, in plain sight, watching Emily clean up the kitchen then move to the living room to pick up her needle work and settle into her straight backed chair by the glowing lamp.

This had been her routine every night of the 10 years they'd been married and it bored him purely senseless. He admired her dedication to her children and home. He admired her ability to shut out sadness. Lord knows, she'd sure had her share of sadness. Burying a husband, her Mama and then baby Lloyd inside of six years would've put some women in their own grave. But not Martha Emily. Emily just tied that wispy blond hair into that tight little knot, flattened that mouth into a thin line, squared those narrow shoulders and brooked no nonsense from man nor beast.

Clarence continued watching the house, hoping to catch a glimpse of Vada or Bill in the shadows of that lamp light. Julia May would already be tucked away in the middle of their double bed. After an hour or so, dark had settled over the countryside like a dusty old blanket. Clarence jumped down from the wagon and started up the rutted path to the house. Nearly to the dark porch, he was startled when Emily called out,

"Where do you think you're going?"

"Hoped to sit down, talk ... maybe have a glass of tea... see the kids."

"No tea left, kids are asleep, nothing to talk about." Clarence continued on then sat down on the porch steps.

"Oh, Emily, Please. I joined the Army today and will be shipping out at noon tomorrow. I hope to learn some new skills, find new job opportunities for when I get back, find a way for a better life for all of us. Can't we just have a little visit? Let me see Vada and Bill. And Julia May. I want to see all of the kids really – Myrt and Virgie, too. But I sorely long to see Bill. I think he'll miss me most and I want him to know that my leaving is for a good reason, a good cause but that I will be back. It has nothing to do with him. He needs to know that I believe he's a good boy and that I love him. He needs to know that I'm proud of him and that I'll be back someday soon."

"Are those words for me or Bill?"

"Just what I said, Em. I need to see Bill before I leave."

"Guess you shoulda thought those thoughts before you took off yesterday. Scaring your children. Caused me to be harsh with them. Caused me to be short with June, even with her already worried senseless over Gordon. You talk him into joining up to keep you company?"

"No, I didn't know he had joined until day before yesterday when we got here to Larue. He enlisted a few days ago and was supposed to leave today but he got all nervous and skittish. The recruiting officer told Slick it would be best if he didn't go but that he should stay here and 'hold the ropes' so to speak. Slick got mad, tore up the papers and walked home from Athens."

"What did he get upset about?"

"He got all upset when he found out that we probably wouldn't be stationed together because of being family. He seemed to panic some." Clarence relaxed against the porch railing but Emily stood ramrod straight.

"See, Emily, it isn't so hard to have a conversation, is it. Now, can't I see the children? Just for a few minutes?"

"This is no conversation – it's you trying to work your charm so you can go off feeling proud of yourself. Telling yourself you have done no harm to anyone. It's not working and NO, you're not seeing the children. You need to get on outta here. Some of us have to get to sleep. There's field work to be done tomorrow."

Clarence stood back up. "Martha Emily, you're a hard woman. Filled with spite and anger. Some of it is understandable. Some of it is just meanness for no reason. You need to remember one thing. You're not hurting me. You're hurting your children, your little boy most of all. You remember THAT." He whirled around, headed back down to the wagon, climbed up then jumped back down from the seat and headed south on foot. South toward the Clark place. Emily knew exactly where he was going.

Neither Clarence nor Emily saw Vada standing in the dark, a few steps back from the front door. They didn't know she'd heard every word. They didn't know that while she watched her Daddy leave, there were big tears falling down her cheeks. They didn't know that she went back to the bedroom she shared with her two older sisters who were also awake and whispered to them,

"Papa's gone. Papa asked to see us but Mama said *No*. He didn't abandon us. He joined the Army and is going to war. But he loves us and will come back to us soon."

Clarence reported for duty the next morning in Athens. Young Corporal was nowhere to be seen. In his place was a burly drill Sergeant that looked like he ate whole raw chickens for breakfast. The room was full with about 20 other area men when Clarence strolled in wearing his best grin. Sgt. Odell spoke, louder than truly necessary, "Private, knock that smile off your face. You won't be needing it for the next six weeks. Besides, you're late and that's nothing to smile about."

"I'm not late. I was due here at noon and its only 11:55am."

"That may be, but you're the last one to arrive. That's the same as LATE. Now sit down and get ready to listen. A nervous hush fell across the room. "At 1300, all you fine young gentlemen will board a train bound for Houston. When you arrive there, you'll load into a caravan heading to Bryan/College Station. There, you will be shown to your home for the next six weeks. You will undergo rigorous field and fitness training, led by the graduate officers of Texas A&M. I will meet you fellows at the chow hall there at 2300 for late mess. From there, you will get your orders for the next day. Any questions? . . . I didn't think so. Now let's move."

Everybody headed toward the door, gathering on the sidewalk, anxious to get underway. Suddenly, the 20 boys seemed confused. "How do we get to the train station from here?"

The railroad depot was no more than a half mile south of the town square but these young recruits were from several counties around East Texas; not just Henderson county.

Sgt. Odell sounded more than a little disgusted when he said, "You've all got two feet. Get a move on." Sgt. flicked his hand-rolled cigarette butt into the street then headed toward the train station. Clarence noticed and thought it a good thing that the butt didn't fall on that creaky old wood sidewalk. Falling into step, the soon-to-be soldiers were a sight to behold. Dressed in everything from worn out overalls to their Sunday go-to-meeting best, the men gave it their untrained all to march in an orderly fashion. Enthusiasm was running high among the men, all eager to go to battle. Clarence kept quiet; his thoughts on the subject of what lay ahead were not quite as grand as those of his new found friends.

Reaching the depot, the group of G.I.s had no time to mingle with the half dozen or so 'working girls' who were loitering in the station. The engineer on the big black locomotive was blowing the steam whistle and the conductor was calling "All aboard! All aboard! This is your Final call for the 1:20 Southbound Interurban passenger train to Houston, Texas." The men rushed up the steps only to find all the seats taken by other excited recruits. They were still standing when the train began lurching forward with jerks that tossed some of them onto the laps of a few surprised seated passengers.

Leaving the station in Athens, the engine picked up speed, rambling through the scorched summer countryside. This time of year, the scenery was mostly brown from the rolling hills to tops of the scrappy Live Oaks and Pines. The conductor stepped into the car, frowned at the crowd standing and herded them across the coupling back into the next passenger car where benches were available for sitting. Lulled into a stupor by the rocking rhythm of the train, but before sleep could set in, the Conductor clattered back into the car, announcing the upcoming stop in Poyner ~ Frankston. Perking up, the boys glanced out, expecting to see a town. They were disappointed to see only an empty platform with a bag of mail sitting near the edge. As the train slowed, the conductor leaned out with a long, hooked metal pole, grabbing the bag. At once, the train began picking up speed again.

This start/slow/start routine jolted the train load of young soldiers throughout the rest of the afternoon and into the evening twilight. They got a glimpse of the Palestine depot but not much else. The ride didn't smooth into a steady clickity-clack until after 8pm. With the boys finally asleep, the conductor came back through shortly after 10 o'clock, this time to make sure the boys knew to gather up for departure. "Ya'll are about to reach Houston where you'll depart."

Clarence spoke what all the guys were thinking. "Where do we go now?"

"You'll find your coaches waiting by the platform for the rest of your journey. God bless you, boys."

Stiff and sore, the men shuffled off the train to find another type of train. They were startled to find a caravan of 25 open topped, wooden wagons with their drivers lined up and ready to roll. Looking around, the Henderson County boys discovered for the first time that they were among a couple of hundred other new recruits, all headed to boot camp. 200 Texas boys left home that day, ready to go to Europe to fight for their country.

As everyone milled around, getting their bearings, Drill Sergeant Odell suddenly appeared. In a voice easily heard above the crowd, he shouted "Well, what are you children waiting for? We're already late and there's hot food ahead."

In groups, as the boys hurriedly began climbing into the wagons, they suddenly realized how long it had been since they last ate. Gradually, the wagon train started to rumble away, leaving the station behind.

Clarence had found a perch on a hay bale toward the front of a wagon bed just behind the driver. This vantage point gave him visibility to the number of men in the training unit. He also could look over his left shoulder and see what lay ahead of the procession. And, he could be seen by Sgt. Odell who was in a wagon toward the end of the long caravan. Clarence felt sure that he was more stable and maybe wiser than some of the young greenhorns. He was a good ten years older than most and he had roamed this part of Texas in his 'bachelor days' so he wasn't as lost.

Clarence's thoughts turned back to last night, spent at Cora's house. Though it seemed like weeks ago, this pleasant memory caused him to ease to a sitting position on the floor of the wagon and relax against the hay. With a half grin on his face and his hat covering his eyes, he dozed. Nearly two hours drifted by peacefully before a commotion stirred him alert. They had reached Bryan/College Station where they were met by a band of uniformed young Aggie officers on horseback. Some of them didn't look old enough to shave. Some of the guys in the wagons started a heckling chant.

But the commanding voice of Sgt. Odell rang out, "Knock it off. Those fine young men are going to teach you how to keep from getting killed. And how to take out a few Krauts as well. Now, you may not like your assigned commanding officer but you will learn from him, come hell or high water. Your life depends on it. And maybe the lives of your mothers, sisters, & sweethearts. So keep your opinions to yourselves. Charlie Clarence Jones... Where are you in this crowd?"

Clarence seemed to appear out of thin air, "Right here, sir."

"Gather your buddies and head on over to the mess hall. Get your trays, find seats but wait for the rest of this unruly mob to get their grub before you set down to chow."

Turning to face the sea of young G.I.s, Sgt. Odell thundered out. "All you recruits, leave your baggage in the wagons and fall in behind Jones here. Listen to what he tells you to do."

Clarence was mobbed with dozens of fresh faces ready to follow orders so he turned to one of the mounted Aggie officers. "Would you mind directing me toward the Mess Hall?"

The First Lieutenant Barry responded firmly, "Don't you mean, "Sir, where is the Mess Hall, Sir?"

Clarence knew how to pick his battles so with a sigh, he answered "Yes, Sir. Where is the Mess Hall, Sir?"

"Look behind you. Just the other side the row of wagons, across the road," came the laughing answer.

Clarence gave no reply but raised his arm, hat in hand, straight up into the air. He strode across the dirt road toward the Mess Hall that actually turned out to be a tent. The biggest tent he'd ever seen in his life. He stopped at the flap door while the hungry men bunched up all around him. Loudly, he repeated Sgt. Odell's instructions. "Get in line, get a tray, get it filled, get a spot at a table but remain standing in place until everyone has their food." Then Clarence added, "I think it would be in all our best interest to obey those orders."

Pulling back the flap and stepping inside, he was hit with all sorts of familiar aromas; wet canvas, mud, sawdust, grease, biscuits, bacon, cast iron skillets, eggs, chicken feathers. The aroma of bacon surfaced strongest of all and Clarence was suddenly starving.

Surprisingly, all 200 men proceeded as asked, lining up, getting full trays, spreading out in the huge tent that could easily hold three times as many.

Sgt. Odell came in, got a tray and joined the table where Clarence and his Athens cohorts were standing. Odell looked around at the men, clustered in groups according to hometown then boomed out, "Bring those trays and move in here, altogether. Close ranks. You will become a unit over the next few weeks. You will learn to think as one. Lean on each other. Trust each other as though your life depends on it. And a time will come for some of you when it will. You will become brothers – might as well start now. Be seated."

The recruits forgot that they were nearly exhausted as they fell into their meal of eggs, bacon, potatoes, buttered biscuits and syrup. Washing it all down with lots of strong, hot coffee, the men were eager to do nothing more than sit in the tent and think about their future.

Sgt. Odell stood up then boomed, "Attention!" Though they didn't know exactly what to do, they all realized that a quick response was in order. Everyone jumped to their feet, a few boys threw up timid salutes which drew snickers from the young Aggie officers who sat together across the mess tent.

Sgt. Odell appreciated the effort and told the boys, "At ease, men. Right now, it's 0200. You all need to go grab your bags and head to the barracks. Find a bunk, put all your belongings away. Maybe catch a little shut eye. Breakfast at 0530 then report to the infirmary by 0700. There you will be inspected for lice, flat feet, dental problems and a several other malformations. You will also receive your first G.I. haircut and be issued uniforms. As soon as you get your gear, go back to the barracks, unload everything and properly stow it away then report to the parade field behind the mess hall. You will meet your company Commanding Officer, First Lieutenant Elkhart. Be there no later than 1100. Dismissed."

Fired up again, the men skirmished like children to get through the flap door then burst out into the pitch dark like toothpaste shot from the tube. Grabbing their baggage, they realized at once that they had no idea where the barracks were. A couple of the ever present Aggie officers were milling nearby. One of the new enlistees asked "Sir, could you tell me where the barracks are, Sir?"

"Sure we can. See the two story brown buildings down the road here? That'll be your home during your stay here at A&M Training. You boys are assigned to the Mayo Barracks Building. You'll love it – when you do get to lie on your bunk. You'll hate it – when it's time to clean the latrine."

Figuring the officers were playing them for fools, they laughed off the 'latrine' comment and headed toward the building. They were greeted with two floors of double rows of single, iron bunk beds, none of which had any bedding, except a bare, thin mattress. There were two metal trunks at the foot of each double bunk. At the far end of the building there was a door marked "Latrine." Curious, the group headed toward the door, peeped through to find a single row of 15 sparkling clean toilets. For some, indoor plumbing was an unknown.

Another group of recruits, boys from Sulphur Springs, clattered through the front door at that moment and starting choosing bunks. The Athens guys decided they'd better get busy and do the same before all the good ones on the ground floor were taken. They fell to the task of putting away the few belongings they'd brought along and then they began to stretch out on those flimsy mattresses. Other groups had joined the boys, many hauling bags up the ladder-like stairs to the 2nd floor. The upstairs clomping noise made the men on the ground floor wonder if they should've picked an upstairs bunk themselves. Soon, the congenial group quieted and the snoring fired up. Clarence put all his belongings in the footlocker, neat as a pin. His one spare shirt went in last. Once everyone else was asleep, he went to the latrine and rinsed out the shirt he had worn that day, wringing it out then smoothing it flat on top of his trunk. At last, he dozed. In the distance, he heard a faint noise like a band going by. But he just rolled over, ignored the noise, threw an arm across his face and didn't open an eye.

The clattering of boots and morning sounds didn't stir Clarence, either, as he made up for some lost sleep. But about 0630, he couldn't ignore his cot shaking as though an earthquake was in full force. Likewise, he could not ignore Thurman Parker yelling in his ear, "You better get a move on. We gotta get to the infirmary in order to be at the parade field on time."

Clarence sat bolt upright, looked around and saw that a few other young soldiers had also slept through breakfast. He was mortified and mumbled a hasty "thanks" to Thurman as he hit the floor at a run. Thurman just grinned as he sauntered toward the door, rattling a dried acorn in his pocket and kicking cots as he went. All the young recruits were now stirring, whispering to each other to "Hurry. You don't want to end up on Clarence's List now do you?" The boys all agreed, for reasons unknown, that nobody wanted to be on Clarence's bad side.

Suddenly, the sleepyheads were high behind, off to the infirmary only to find themselves waiting with about 50 other fellow stragglers who had been on the train. Oh, well, somebody had to be last. Guys were trickling out, done with the medical checkup, the haircut and getting their new clothes. Most of these fellows had a dazed look to go along with the shaved head. None of them had anything to say. They just headed back to the barracks to put away their new G.I. paraphernalia.

One of the new Privates noted that "Those boys who got on in here and are done now will have time to rest a little before gathering at 11 o'clock for whatever we're going to do next. Or was it 1 o'clock? I'm confused with this time thing." An Aggie officer overheard the conversation and said, "Rookie, you're in the Army now. That's 1300, not 1 o'clock.

"Broad as it is long," mumbled the kid. At just that moment, Clarence appeared and, leaning close to boy, whispered "True but you're gonna want to keep that thought to yourself – at least until we get through with this boot camp exercise."

At that same moment, Thurman walked up, looked at Clarence and said, "You're from Athens, right? I'm Thurman Parker, also from Athens – well, Brownsboro right there in Henderson County. I'm having a heck of a time remembering not to smart off to these fancy Soldier Boys. How about we stick together during this training? Maybe you can help me keep my mouth closed!"

Clarence replied, "Might be nice to work alongside somebody from home but I'm making no promises on teaching you to keep your trap shut." Thurman Parker grinned a quiet sly smile but said nothing else. He just slowed his pace to keep in step with Clarence and kept rattling the acorn that he always had in a pocket.

Reaching the door of the supply office/infirmary/barber shop, Clarence stepped inside to the first stop; the camp barber's chair. Everyone got the same identical haircut. Not so much a cut as it was a shearing. All the men left the chair with nothing more than a shadow on their heads and feeling like a sheep being readied for slaughter.

Clarence didn't mind the haircut. He figured it would be easier during training in the August heat. Clarence held no notion that training would be any sort of a good time. He thought of it as something to be endured. Pretty much the same way he looked at farming or raising all those children. He wouldn't miss that at all – except for his boy, Bill. He already sort of missed Bill. Yes, boot camp training was merely a 'next step' to whatever was in his future. A life Clarence sorely hoped would not include so much dirt.

Moving on from the haircut station, Clarence was checked for flat feet, a curved spine, a ticking heart. His teeth, eyes and fingers and toes were counted. He was proud to be found healthy enough to get shot at and sleep in a ditch. Clarence moved to the next stop and received three uniforms; One consisted of a khaki shirt, brown britches, black brogan boots, a braided belt, a black tie and a brown Garrison hat. The other two uniforms were also brown khaki shirts of a coarse material with matching pants that were heavy enough to use for an emergency shelter, heavy black work boots, another woven belt, four pairs of skivvies and four pairs of wool socks. All the boys were issued sheets, a green wool blanket and the world's flatest pillow, made of gray striped cotton ticking. Plus, they got safety razors, combs, toothbrushes, soap, a couple of washcloths, an aluminum hand warmer, a canteen, a three pound flashlight and one towel. They were also issued a good-sized green, canvas duffle bag that, when fully packed and slung across their shoulders, looked like they were smuggling a small body.

Loaded like a pack mule, Clarence waited on Thurman who had entered into the process flow just behind him. As it turned out, Thurman didn't go on to the infirmary right after breakfast. He'd held up to go with his new best friend. Shortly, Thurman emerged into the sunlight beneath his own load of possessions. The two men staggered awkwardly back to the barracks and to their bunks, dumping the load onto their old worn mattresses. A couple of the Aggie officers who were milling around the room approached and told them to make up their beds and put their Issue in the locker. Clarence threw his pile down and got to work, first he set in folding and sorting everything except the bedding and stacking it all into the trunk along with his personal things that he's already stowed. Then, he moved the sheets and covers over to the bunk. He snapped the first sheet out flat then began folding and tucking corners. Top sheet came next, the bottom corners finished tight as a drum. Finally, the tank green wool blanket was added, tucked only at the bottom with the bulk folded back, flat accordion style. As Clarence stood back to admire his handiwork, the Aggie officers loitered by the door watching him. One whispered to the other, "He's got the potential of being a good NCO." To which his buddy answered, "Yeah, he's either going to be a good soldier or a royal pain in the ass."

By 1045, all the men had been pronounced healthy, shorn of excess hair and were in possession of their new Army wardrobe. They deposited the load in the bunks and made their way to the mess tent, still dressed in civilian clothes.

By 11 o'clock – make that 1100, all 200 of the men were milling in back of the mess hall tent. There had been nowhere near a full night's sleep and a couple of meals, so many of them were half asleep on their feet. A Lt. Elkhart stood just inside the mess tent, looking out at the newest bunch of eager recruits. He shrugged, shook his head and stepped outside, moving toward a podium at the far end of a football field sized clearing surrounded by the tall trees of the Piney Woods.

Sgt. Odell sprang out of the tent and bellowed "Fall In!" Unsure of what they should do, the young men lined up next to each other and stood quiet and still. Only a few renegades snickered. Clarence and Thurman lined up side by side, straight arrows facing forward. While not in a formal 'attention' stance, they were on full alert and focused. Sgt. Odell took notice as Lt. Elkhart began to speak.

"Welcome boys. Welcome to my command at Kyle Field, here at Texas A&M. Over the next six weeks, you will become soldiers. No longer boys, you will become men of honor, courage and patriotism. You will number among the almost one million Americans who have already volunteered to help win this war that will end wars forever. I don't know what your expectations are but I'm here to tell you, this is not summer camp. You will be trained by the toughest, strictest, harshest, most dedicated ~ the BEST ~ Army soldiers in the world – Texas A&M Aggies. You will work harder, in worse conditions, than you've ever seen in your life. You will learn to rely on your wits, your intuition, and the guy lying next to you in the trench. You will learn to shoot a rifle and load artillery. You will get used to being hungry, to ignoring wet socks and cold feet. And yet, when you leave here, you still will not be fully prepared for what you'll experience in a war zone under attack. A few of you will learn to be platoon leaders and some of you may even make careers in the military. But most will be foot soldiers – a profession full of discipline and pride – and you'll be back on the farm in a year or two. But I'm sorry to say, some of you won't come back. That statement is not meant to scare you or sound dramatic. It is meant to emphasize how important it is for you to pay attention to what these training officers teach you.

Enough chat. Some of you look like you could use a bath then a hot meal. Or a nap. Cookie has the midday meal ready so, this time, you get to choose. Eat or hit the bunks. Either way, show up for evening chow, dressed in those new khakis by 1700. Dismissed."

Nobody wanted to miss a meal so the boys scrambled into mess, grabbed a tray and took what Cook dished out. They didn't notice until they sat down that they had fried bologna, scrambled eggs with water gravy and biscuits. This was fine home cooking for many of the boys. They ate hurriedly, figuring there would be lines for the showers in those small latrines. For some, this was the first indoor bath they'd had in their lives – and they quite liked it! In less than an hour, though, every last man was freshly showered and stretched out on their chosen bunk. Let the snoring begin, at 1400 – 2 o'clock in the afternoon!

Tired to the bone, still Clarence lay awake. He wasn't worried so much about what the future might hold once he got to Europe; He was thinking about coming back home to Emily and the kids when it was over. Just about the time he dozed off, boots began hitting the floor above his head. That heavy clomping would prove to be the most effective alarm clock ever.

The only hesitation any of the men had was which of the newly issued shoes they should wear to supper. Clarence chose his boots and was heading toward the door when Thurman caught up with him.

Thurman grinned and said "You think there'll be meat for supper?" Thurman Parker grew up in a large family of seven siblings with farm laborer parents. They followed the crops from East Texas to California and back seasonally. There was always plenty of vegetables on the table but not much meat. When there was, it was usually just about enough for five kids so the seven of them always had to wrestle for a serving, after their daddy got finished. Now, Thurman couldn't get enough meat – beef, pork, venison – he really didn't care. But, oh, how he loved bacon!

Clarence answered, "I do. I've read that they want us to have 4,000 calories per day during training so that we'll gain a bit of weight, at first. Then later when we don't have much to eat, we'll have a little extra fat to live off of."

"Clarence, you have a way of beating the fun out of everything. I was just making conversation on the walk to supper. I don't much care for the idea of being fattened up for slaughter."

Clarence sighed as he opened the flap door to the mess tent. Wonderful aromas greeted them again. Falling into line to pick up their metal trays, Thurman grinned. "I smell beef. I'm a meat and potatoes kinda guy."

Clarence snickered, "You don't say!"

Both sat down with the other Athens boys as everyone began eating. Roast beef, rice and gravy, corn, carrots, rolls. Even bread pudding which made Clarence smile and think of Slick with his sweet tooth. Enough for seconds all around. As the clinking metal utensil noise slowed down, Sgt. Odell stood. He waited for all the men to fall silent and pay attention before he spoke:

"Time to call it a night, boys. Today has been a fun day at camp. Tomorrow, training begins. Report back here in the morning at 0500, dressed out. Bring your duffle. Load up all your new issue, including your blanket & pillow – Everything except that fine Army mattress. After breakfast, at 0600 sharp, field maneuvers begin. The Aggie officers will be in charge of the units; I will be responsible for assignments and will hear their comments on your progress. I will report directly to Lt. Commander Elkhart. You will communicate only with the officer in charge of your unit – and each other. At the end of six weeks, you will be ready for battle – or you will be ready to go home. Now let's get some real sleep..... Oh, one last thing: Leave the Cook alone – no whining about the food, no begging or bribing for seconds. Cook holds your future well-being by the ladle."

By the end of the second week of October, the temperature at night had cooled to the mid-70s. On October 11, 1916 Clarence graduated from U.S. Army boot camp at Texas A&M in Bryan/College Station. The class gathered one last time on the parade field behind the mess tent. The men were not recognizable as the same scraggly, scared boys that first met there six weeks before. Today, there were 194 men assembled, ready to go to battle for the U.S. of A. Only six fellows failed to make the grade and were sent home early by Lt. Elkhart – All of the Athens boys, including Clarence, were still standing. The men were eager to get home for the five day leave they were granted; eager to show off for their families. They had almost a week before reporting back to the base to receive destination orders.

To no one's surprise, Clarence had graduated close to the top of the class. Everyone figured Clarence would draw some cushy office assignment since all the men learned that a dirty was the biggest enemy as far as Clarence was concerned. Clarence's future duty was the main gossip topic as the men climbed onto the wagon caravan to Houston then onboard the trains heading north.

On arrival in Athens, Thurman thumped Clarence on the shoulder with a "Hidey Ho, Old Man – See you in five for the return to hell," as he whistled off, rattling the ever-present acorn in his pocket. With a little grin, Clarence dipped his cap, straightened his tie and headed across the platform, out the front of the station. There sat Slick and June, waiting to give Clarence a ride back to the house. Slick jumped down, faced Clarence and presented a jaunty little half salute.

"Well, just look at you! Don't you look sharper than a little rat pill. Junie, maybe we shoulda hired a carriage to fetch Clarence here."

June watched a shadow flit across Clarence's face so she said "Hush it, Slick."

Clarence tossed his duffel into the wagon then climbed in. "How's everything been? Farming okay? How's Bill? And Emily? And Vada and Julia May? And the girls??

Slick replied, "Farm is d-d-doing fine. Everybody is good. Emily is her usual s-self. K-K-Kids are growing like weeds. Even B-B-Bill though he st-ill ain't very tall. Then, again, you-you ain't, either! Wa-HaHaHa!"

June slipped her hand through Slick's arm and said, "You've only been gone six weeks, Clarence. Not a lot has around here has changed. *You're* the one who has changed."

With a shrug, Clarence asked, "Does Emily know I'm coming home?"

June, "She knows you're coming back to town on leave for a week, yes."

Clarence knew then that he'd have to work to talk his way back home and to see the children. "Will it be all right if I rest up awhile when we get to y'all's house? Been a long day on the train. I'll go see Emily and the kids in a little bit. If it's okay?"

Slick spoke up. "Course it is. June m-m-made up the spare room for you to use while you're home. S-S-Supper will be ready soon after we get in, right J-J-Junie?

June glanced at Slick but didn't say anything, just gripped his arm a little tighter. Not much else was said the rest of the ride to the DeHart place.

True to Slick's word, supper was ready within the hour after Clarence toted his duffel into the bedroom. June had cooked that morning so it was just a matter of setting the table. Meatloaf and mashed potatoes, the last of the summer squash, fresh greens, cornbread and blackberry pie. He had forgotten what a great cook June was.

After eating all he could stand, Slick stood then picked his plate up, taking it to the sink. Surprised, Clarence did the same. "Thank you for that marvelous supper, June. You have no idea how good that all tasted. Six weeks of watery dried eggs, powdered milk and smoked fatback will ruin a feller." Then, he walked out in to the backyard toward the barn, sitting down on a ancient tree stump worn smooth from wood chopping and rolled a cigarette. Slick didn't follow him out because June said, "Just let him be, Gordon. Give him a chance to breath."

LEAVE THE LAMP ON...

Clarence just sat. Sat and rested his still blistered feet. Sat and watched the glowing orange sun sink into the western horizon. Sat and thought about his duty assignment which wouldn't be announced until he got back to post at Bryan next week. Sat and thought about what his future might hold after finishing this military duty. But mostly, he just sat. He smoked that rolled cigarette, a newly acquired habit and one that Clarence was not sure he wanted to continue. Suddenly, he realized that the sun had slipped behind the trees down by the creek and before long, dark would soon be replacing the dusky light. Standing up from the stump, Clarence called back into the kitchen. "Slick, okay if I take the wagon? I want to go on down to see Emily and the kids now."

"Y-Y-You know it is. Just be smart. She missed you but you know she ain't gonna let on. I expect to find the wagon – and you – back here in the morning."

"Sir, Yes, Sir!" replied Clarence. Slick grinned and heaved out a deep breath that he hadn't realized he'd been holding.

Clarence went back into the house; made sure his uniform still looked presentable then bolted out across the yard to the barn. Leading the horses out, he had them harnessed and hitched up in record time. He waved at Slick and headed out.

Drawing up out in the road in front of the house, he stopped to watch the children move from room to room. He saw the girls helping clean up the kitchen and Vada holding Julia May, feeding her tidbits from the table. At last, he saw Bill pass through the light. He looked like he'd grown four inches in the last six weeks!

Clarence continued to sit, watching, waiting, wondering. He waited long enough for the light to go out in the kitchen and the lamp to come on in the living room. Again, he could see Emily sitting by the light with her never-ending handwork. He jumped off the wagon and started across the yard. Emily met him on the bottom porch step. "What do you want?"

"I just want to see you and the children. I want to talk a little bit. I want to say I'm sorry for how I left before. I want you to know what my plan was – and still is. I want to make sure that I'll be welcomed back home when the war is over. I ship out for Europe real soon."

Emily was glad to see Clarence. She wanted to give him a hug and for him to hug her back but there was no way under the moon or stars that she was about to let on that he'd been missed. "Boot camp sure didn't change you any. You're still the same old Clarence. Everything is all about you. Do you even care that your kids have missed you every day? Bill talks about "my Daddy" like you're a saint. Julia

May even cries in her sleep some nights, mumbling "Pap, Pap." And Vada . . . I have no idea what she's thinking. She doesn't talk to me about anything. It's as though her light has been blown out. Myrt and Virgie – well, they've lost a daddy before. They know it's not the end of the world and so they just keep plugging along every day.

So . . . you're shipping out are you? When? Where you going? For how long?"

Clarence thought he felt a glimmer of hope in Emily with her questions. That just maybe she would let him come back. He told her, "Yes, I go back to Bryan/College Station next week. I'll get my marchin' orders from Lt. Elkhart – the base commander – then. We're not supposed to know anything yet about where we're being sent. But Sgt. Odell gave me a hint that I'll be on a troop ship, crossing the Atlantic, landing in France, some place called Saint-Nazaire – wherever that might be. I was hoping that you'd see fit to let me come back home for the week. Let me make it up to you for the way I behaved back in August."

"Humph. Let you come back so that the children can get used to you being here and then you up and leave again. I don't think so. How cruel can you be?"

Clarence stood silent for a moment, thinking that what she said did make some little bit of sense. "I get it, Emily. I really do. But, I think I could help them understand that I'm going to serve our country. It's a duty that men have. They would at least know that I'm not going just for fun or a change of scenery. They would know that this is a sacrifice for them – and you."

Emily never wavered. "Nice talk. You should be a politician. No, you're not setting foot in this house again. You moved us here but never intended to stay or put down roots...so go. Go now. And don't come back again."

Clarence looked at tiny, pale Emily in the dim light filtering out from the lamp in the front room. He knew her path had been hard and rocky. He also knew that he hadn't helped. But how in the world had she become so rigid and unforgiving. He reached into his pocket and took out some folded up cash, holding the bills out to her. "Here, Emily. Take this. I'm getting paid regular now. $1.00 a day so there's more than $40 there. If I get sent to Europe, it'll be even more so I can provide for you and the kids."

"I don't want your money."

"It's OUR money, Martha Emily! That's why I joined up. I've told you that over and over. I enlisted so that you and the kids could have nicer school clothes and shoes that fit – maybe a few trinkets from time to time. Just take the money."

"No. We're doing just fine."

"How can you possibly say that? I've only been gone six weeks. You haven't survived a winter yet, Emily. A season of having to live off what's been stored up. How do you think you'll put up enough to feed 5 growing children for the winter? A season with nothing coming in? You can't chop enough wood to sell for all that? How, Emily? HOW?" Clarence's tone was rising as his aggravation surfaced and his patience dwindled.

Clarence tossed the money down onto the porch then turned away, walking back toward the wagon. He was at his wits end with Emily and couldn't stand there, trying to reason with her any longer. He had to go before he started really yelling and scared little Bill and baby Julia May.

Yet again, neither Emily nor Clarence noticed Vada hovering in the shadows just inside the front door, listening to every word. Vada ached to yell, "Papa, wait. I believe you. I believe you're going to be the finest soldier to ever fight for this country. I believe you never meant to hurt us." But Vada knew better than to do any such thing. She was sure that her mother would put her out and never miss her. Same as she didn't miss Papa. So nine year old Vada stayed in the shadows as hot tears rolled down her cheeks. She watched her Papa climb into the wagon then head back toward Uncle Slick and Aunt June's place. Maybe she'd slip out later, sneak off down the road to hug her Papa before he went so far away to that war she heard the men in town talking about.

Emily stood stock still; ramrod straight, no change in expression as she watched Clarence leave. She longed for Clarence to turn around, look back at her. But he didn't . . . and she would rather choke than give in and call out to him. So she just stood and watched. When she turned to go inside, she caught a glimpse of Vada's skirt as she ran across the front room toward the bedroom.

Waiting for more than an hour until she heard her sisters' whiffling soft snores, Vada quietly opened the bedroom window then stuck her head out to look around. There was only a quartermoon shining so the yard and road were pitch dark. Crickets and tree frogs were the only sounds that floated up to meet her as she leaned out. Never afraid of the dark, Vada pulled up the hem of her nightgown to swing a leg over then drop to the ground. Just as she cleared both legs and perched on the sill ready to leap, a hand gripped her shoulder. Emily quietly hissed, "That's not your best idea, there, Vada Viola. Get back in here and explain yourself. Before you get the whuppin' of your life."

Vada turned back into the room then stepped to the floor. Emily reached to grab Vada's arm but she jerked away from her grip then moved out of reach. Vada said,

"You can threaten and punish me all you want, Mama. But you're not going to hit me anymore. It's not my fault that Papa enlisted to fight in a war to get away from here."

Emily gasped. Stunned not so much by Vada's words but more that she had the gumption to defy her so boldly. Emily stared at Vada in silence. No words exchanged, just looks of shock on both their faces. Vada was as taken aback as Emily. She had never spoken to her mother in such a brazen tone. It had never crossed her mind to do such a thing. Vada figured that her mother's wrath would rain down on her like a hail storm in the spring.

"Vada, you get back in that bed and you keep your mouth shut. I don't want to ever hear you speak of your Papa again. And you will not to talk to your sisters or Bill about him, either. In the morning, you get up and get breakfast ready for Myrt and Virgie so they can get to school. Then, get Bill fed and send him out to tend the chickens and look for eggs. Bathe Julia May and get her fed. I've got the fields ready and Uncle Gordon will be here to help get those beets in the ground. You can plant right alongside us."

"But Mama, I need to get to school, too."

"You'll go next week, maybe."

Vada made up her mind in that moment that she would do two things with her life. First, she would never again worry about making her mother mad; second, she would finish school and leave home as soon as possible. Vada completed 8th grade. Emily allowed Bill to go to school only until he finished the 5th grade then she kept him home to work the farm to feed the family. He was 11 years old.

But Charlie Clarence Jones was gone from their lives forever. At least as far as Vada, Bill and all the rest of the children were concerned.

On October 17th, 1916, Clarence reported back to Camp in Bryan/College Station where he, along with the 194 other men in his new platoon, learned what the Army intended for him to do for the foreseeable future. Charlie would not be heading to France like he'd been led to believe. Instead, he would stay behind at Kyle Field to get additional training. He would be going to Europe later, as a Company Clerk, responsible for ordering supplies and rations and, in general, maintaining order. He would be assigned to Sgt. Odell, joining his old platoon already in Italy. Clarence had two more months before he shipped out so even this assignment could change by then. He couldn't help but think that he'd lucked out with this duty since he thought it would keep him out of the trenches, and mud, that most of the other guys would have to endure.

Over the next eight weeks, Clarence learned how to order everything from wool socks to powdered milk to artillery shells and tanks. He learned how to keep ledgers of when supplies were ordered, from whom and in what quantity. He learned how to issue his own purchase orders when the Commander's secretary was unavailable. He figured out how to shorten the delivery cycle and how to sweet talk the clerks who worked for the government vendors. He also learned to eavesdrop on conversations around him at mess then anticipate the 'needs' that he'd overheard mentioned. In short, Clarence learned how to be indispensable to the officers and the soldiers alike.

After this specialized training was complete, Clarence got another week's leave so he headed back to Athens. This time, he went alone since his buddy Thurman Parker had already left for duty in Italy. Once again, Slick and June met him at the train and took him home with them for the stay. He waited a couple of days before going to Emily's to try to see the children. Surely, she'd let him see them this time since it was so very close to Christmas.

This time, Clarence walked the mile from Slick's to Emily's figuring to avoid even the wagon noise. Emily knew he was there since Slick *was* her brother and he wasn't about to let her get caught off guard by a surprise visit from Clarence. She'd spent the last two nights sitting in the dark living room, waiting. She didn't even turn on the lamp.

Sure enough, on the third night, about midnight, Emily heard the wooden steps creak under the weight of boots. She leapt to the door and threw it open, springing out onto the porch like a cat. "I told you never to come back here, Charlie Clarence Jones. Shouldn't you be in Europe somewhere ... 'Fighting for your country?'"

Showing no surprise, Clarence replied, "I didn't come to argue with you, Emily. I only came to see the kids."

"So why do you always show up in the middle of the night? A decent father would want his children to get enough sleep to do their schoolwork..."

Clarence stiffened, interrupting with "If I'm to believe your own brother, you've been keeping the kids out of school whenever you please. Making them work like field hands."

"I've got a farm to run, mouths to feed."

Clarence took an envelope out of his khaki pocket, held it out to Emily. She reached as if to take it then let it fall to the wooden porch planks.

"Don't be such a mule head, Emily. Christmas is less than a week away – do something for the kids and yourself. There's enough there for a tree and a big dinner.

You could even do something nice for Slick and June. A Thank You for all they've done for you."

Emily huffed, "They don't need anything done for them. They have each other. That's enough." Clarence knew right then why Emily stayed mad all the time – envy. And he felt lower than a snake's belly. Without another word, Clarence turned and left – again.

As soon as he was out of sight, Emily picked up the envelope, glancing into it; she was startled to see eight $20 bills. She went back in the house to the kitchen where she tossed the envelope into the oven, threw in a piece of kindling and a match then watched it burn. Vada stood silently at the end of the kitchen counter, watching Emily. This time, Vada didn't hide from her mother.

Clarence whiled away his few days in Athens at a leisurely pace, passing time at Cora's and at Slick's, enjoying June's cooking. He sure wished he could hug the kids and wish them a Merry Christmas. But he didn't go back to the house again because he didn't want to stir up a scene that could ruin what little happiness they might be allowed to have during the approaching holidays.

Clarence then boarded the train back to Bryan on December 22nd. There, he learned from Lt. Elkhart that he would be joining Sgt. Odell, still in Italy. This was alright with Clarence since he would be located some distance away from the serious battle zones. What rattled him was that he would be en route on December 25th; sooner than he'd expected. It seemed like the training and preparation was too short, that there was too much he still didn't know.

Nevertheless, Clarence found himself in Houston, boarding an airplane for the first time in his life. The uneven, loud roar and shaking race down the runway did nothing to settle him his nerves for the long journey ahead. Soon though, he got up the courage to look out the porthole style window and was surprised to see nothing but water – the view did not change for the next 10 hours except when night fell and he could see nothing at all. The plane noise continued - a loud, angry roar that sort of lulled Clarence into a stupor but did not really put him to sleep. The occasional bounce was unnerving but since no one else reacted to it, he didn't, either.

When at last, the plane landed in Milan, Clarence stepped down onto the tarmac and was met by Sgt. Odell's driver, Private Rossi, a short, slight young man who fairly bled nervous jumpy energy. Private Rossi greeted him in ragged Italian, "Ciao, Benvenuto, Senore".... Clarence could tell that the Private was no more Italian than he was so he said, "Hey, Private. I'm no 'senore' ... I'm a buck private, same as you. Where you from and where're we going?

"I hail from Paris . . . Texas, that is. Sgt. Odell has us trying to learn to speak a few words of Italian, especially out in public, so we don't stand out in the crowd quite so much. I don't think it's working. We're headed up to meet Odell at camp near Varese, near the border with Austria. He's been waiting for you to get here before deciding where we'll go next. He seems to think you're some kind of good luck charm. I sure hope he's right."

"I don't know anything about being a good luck charm. In fact, that's pretty doubtful. Seems that I generally have just the opposite effect on most people. How long you been here?"

Rossi pointed him toward a waiting Jeep as he replied, "I came over with Sgt. Odell and the platoon. I was in your training class back in Bryan/College Station. You were just too pre-occupied to notice most of your fellow recruits."

Somewhat taken aback by that comment, but Clarence just shook his head and asked, "Say, is Thurman Parker here? He was in our class at Bryan."

"Yes, he's here. But he's out in the field. Not in camp like you'll be. From what is going round on the grapevine, you've got a pretty cushy assignment compared to a ditch or a foxhole. No idea how I got so lucky with my job in the motor pool."

"Me, neither. For myself... not you, Rossi! Say, how long is this drive we're on? This Jeep can beat the liver out of you.

"About 30 miles but the road is pretty shot. Artillery hits and tanks – and boots. It'll take about four hours. Your ribs will be sore tomorrow – and probably your butt, too. Look in the box in the back seat if you're hungry. There are some shoe leather sandwiches and hot, boiled motor oil which Cook tries to pass off as coffee. Beats K-rations, though, I guess. And, yes, Cook came along from Bryan, too."

"Thanks, maybe later. You want one?"

"No, I've already had enough for today."

The two privates hung onto the bouncing Jeep, trying to stay inside the iron frame without breaking a rib, flailing along in companionable silence for most the ride. Once in a while, Clarence noticed a burned out shell of a house but Rossi was right, the road was an absolute nightmare of potholes and rub board ridges but the countryside was lovely and serene. He laughed aloud once when he spotted a dark haired little boy about six, running barefoot across a field carrying a bucket and a short handled hoe. Clarence saw flashes of Bill playing in the garden when the hoe handle was two feet longer than he was tall. Bill digging up potatoes though the work was too hard for most children twice his size.

Rossi wanted to know what was funny. Clarence told him about seeing the child and the memory of little Bill, his only son. Rossi asked, "You know what he's doing, don't cha?"

"Hoeing weeds, I guess. What else could it be?"

"He's searching for landmines. Pray that he doesn't find any."

Clarence spun around, staring back at the farmhouse and the little boy in the distance. He felt a rock land in the pit of his stomach.

Arriving in camp long after dark, Clarence's knees almost buckled when he got out of the Jeep. The effects of 14 hours on an airplane then four hours in that hard-riding, teeth jarring killer mobile had taken a toll. In addition to being almost totally stove up as if he were 80 years old, he was covered in grit from the open air ride through the Italian countryside. He didn't want to go with Rossi to Sgt. Odell's field office but he knew not to disobey orders.

Sgt. Odell was deep in conversation with a Captain when Clarence and Rossi stepped into the small tent. They stopped, waiting for the huddled conversation to finish and then be acknowledged.

The Captain glanced up and immediately stopped talking when he saw the two Privates. Sgt. Odell stood, greeted Clarence then introduced him to Capt. Stutz. "Well, hey there old man. Sure good to see you. How was the trip? Rossi here treat you okay? Did he feed you?"

"The trip was fine. I lived through the plane ride. Rossi was a very good driver considering we were in a gasoline powered buckboard, traveling on roads that need to be plowed under. And yes, he did offer me food which I declined. Regretfully. I'm hoping there may be some leftovers in the mess tent."

Captain Stutz had had enough of this "old buddy o'mine" greeting, especially for a rank Private who'd already been given way too much special treatment, to his way of thinking. "Mess tent is not open 24 hours a day. It does not provide menu service or hold 'leftovers' for midnight snacks. I'd suggest you hit the cot and be ready to fall out for breakfast at 0500 – *if* we get to spend a full night at rest."

"Fine, Sir. Would somebody point me toward the barracks and I'll be happy to oblige, Sir."

"Barracks? Odell, you better set this private straight. Barracks! He is clearly confused about where he is and what for! This is not a vacation.... It is war. He is a foot soldier and he better learn that right off the bat."

Sgt. Odell gave Clarence a quick look then said, "Private Jones, bunking is in tents as we are a mobile platoon, frequently moving, on foot, through the woods. We scout ahead alongside the roadway whenever possible so that equipment and supplies can be trucked safely to the new bivouac locations. Often, movement is at night so when you get a chance to catch some shut eye on a cot rather than a ditch, take it. See you at breakfast. Private Rossi here will show you where to settle in. That will be all."

Rossi: "Let's go. Grab your duffle." Once outside, back to the Jeep, Rossi said, "Guess that came as a surprise. Sgt. is not running the show here. Non-Coms aren't in charge once you leave boot. Capt. Stutz is a lot of hot air but when push comes to shove, he'll have your back. We'll probably be here at least through tomorrow then maybe break camp the next day. Who knows? So ... Go to bed. Reveille will roll us all out at 0430, mess opens at 0500. You'll report back to Sgt's field office at 0530 for duty assignments. Don't look so worried. I got you covered. All of us good ol' Texas boys gotta stick together, you know."

"Thanks, Rossi. I appreciate your help already," Clarence was sincere. He quietly slipped into the large tent where Rossi led him and was surprised – again – to find only four other privates already asleep inside. He stumbled to an empty cot, grateful that it was fully made up with sheets and a blanket, dumped his duffle and stripped off his clothes. Only then did he realize that Rossi didn't show him a shower or latrine. As much as he hated the thought, he fell onto the bed without scrubbing off the grit.

In only seconds, Clarence was snoring. One of his bunk mates hurled a pillow in his general direction with an oath on the breeze right behind it. Shortly after that, the bugler rang out with a rousing chorus of Reveille and the camp grudgingly began to stir. Slowly and stiffly, Clarence hit the ground, intent on finding a shower.

Stumbling outside, Clarence found a crowd of hungry grumps all headed toward the mess tent. To his surprise, most of the men were only partially dressed, most in just boots, fatigues and white, cotton Fruit of the Loom undershirts. Abandoning the idea of a morning shower, he joined the breakfast parade. Unlike the men in basic training, these guys didn't wait for anyone else to grab a tray, sit down or say grace. Everyone fell to eating as though they hadn't had a meal in days. Clarence later learned that some of them had only eaten meat rations, or canned bully beef, for the last week. While that would keep body and soul together, it was hardly a balanced, or tasty, diet. They were thrilled to be back in reach of a field kitchen.

Clarence had never been a picky eater but he wasn't one to take on large amounts at a single sitting. With a tray of only 2 scrambled, powdered eggs, 2 pieces of bacon, and a hard tack biscuit, Clarence drew some stares as he joined a table of fellows who looked vaguely familiar. One enlisted man muttered, "Thought you'd be sitting with them officer dudes." Puffing up but before he had a chance to respond, Clarence felt a hand on his shoulder as Rossi scooted in next to him then announced, "As soon as you get done, Capt. Stutz wants to see you."

Then he whispered, "Actually, he wants to see both of us, along with Sgt. Odell. But there's no need for these clod-heads here to know that." Clarence glanced down into his breakfast and added some speed to his eating. "I'll meet you there. Gotta go get cleaned up and dressed."

Rossi replied to Clarence, "Be there by 0700" then to the rest of the guys at the table when Clarence left the tent, "Lighten up. He's an okay fellow. Just a little older than most of us and with a calmer head, maybe. At any rate, the officers seem to like him and besides that, he's got a purchase order book to supply anything we need. You'd be smart to stay on his good side." With that, Rossi picked up his empty tray and skedaddled out of mess to make sure he got to the Officer's Field unit before Clarence.

Clarence reported to the Officers Unit at 0658, finding Capt. Stutz and Sgt. Odell in the same position, and what appeared to be the same conversation, which they were in last night. Rossi about ran up his back leg when he stopped just inside the tent opening. Capt.'s demeanor was much warmer than last night though. "Come on in, Private Jones. Have a seat here. Rossi, wait outside, would you. Don't allow any loitering about."

"We've received orders to break camp and move northwest. We'll leave in seven days so there'll be ample time to stock up on everything needed for at least a 30 day march. You'll be responsible for checking inventory, determining what is needed; then, getting orders placed so delivery can be made. We're depending on you to perform as you've been trained. You'll let me know when we're stocked and ready to roll.

One other thing, Private. You're not to speak of this move to anyone yet. We don't need word to spread through the ranks that might leak to the locals in town. We're close enough to Austria and Germany for 'big ears' to be around about."

"I appreciate the trust you're placing in me. And I'll do my very best not to let you, or Sgt. Odell, down. But might I call on a fellow recruit for some help. Someone who would respect the situation and keep quiet?" Rossi had remained within two feet of the tent flap so, upon hearing Clarence's request, his chest pumped up like a balloon at a kid's birthday party.

Capt. replied, "Of course, you'll need a right hand to keep up with records, delivery, etc. Who do you have in mind?"

"Private Thurman Parker. He was in my graduating class in Texas. We practically grew up together. He's a straight arrow kind of guy."

Still listening, Rossi deflated like that same balloon.

Capt. Stutz called out, "Private Rossi, find Private Parker. Tell him he's needed here, on the double."

Disappointed, sort of embarrassed and just a little bit mad, Rossi still took off at a trot to find Private Parker, running back to the mess tent and shouting inside "Thurman Parker... If you're in here, speak up. If you're not, keep quiet!" Nobody answered.

Next, Rossi headed down the row to the first barracks tent where he burst inside, shouting "Parker." Nothing. On to the 2nd and 3rd tent with the same results. Not only was Thurman missing. So was everyone else. Guess they were all still in the makeshift latrines.

Finally, bursting into the 4th tent down the row, Rossi located Thurman, still asleep. Rossi couldn't speak. He was gasping so hard for air that he felt as though he was about to burst a lung. The wheezing was loud enough to wake Thurman who rose up on one elbow, opened an eye and grumbled, "This better be important."

Rossi was still out of breath and in no mood for another surly Private, "It IS. Get your lazy behind out of that bed and get over to Capt. Stutz's tent. Pronto!"

"Who?"

This was more than Rossi could calmly handle. He pulled up to his full height of 5 feet, 3 inches to stand almost at attention, drew a ragged deep breath then answered in a growl, "Capt. Stutz is your commanding officer here in the field and he wants you in the HQ tent immediately."

Now wide awake and in motion, Parker grabbed his khakis from across the foot of the cot and his boots, all in one movement. "Why didn't you say so to start with?" Thurman snatched up a clean undershirt and headed to the latrine.

Rossi just shook his head and left the bunk area to go to find his own platoon leader.

Thurman let no grass grow under him as he hastily dressed, making sure he had that ever present acorn in his pocket, then took off at a trot to find this Capt. Stutz fellow's tent. He was taken aback to find Clarence Jones seated at a portable desk with papers strewn all around while Sgt. Odell and Capt. Stutz (he guessed based on the brass stripes) hovered over him, talking about routes.

Clarence looked rather bewildered when he glanced up but greeted him like a lost brother, "Thurman Parker, you old dog. Ain't you a sight for sore eyes? How you been getting on here? Working hard or hardly working?"

"Harder than you, I'd guess. Look at that spotless uniform and clean fingernails. Why, you're even freshly shaved! You just sitting there shoving papers around. Is that what they trained you special for?" Thurman grinned, really happy to see that friendly familiar face.

"I was enjoying a good rest, in a bed, for the first time in two weeks when your little buddy woke me up to report to a Capt. Stutz. Why do I get the feeling that you, Clarence, are behind that little surprise?"

Capt. Stutz spoke up, "You'd be right about that, Private. Jones here will be working around the clock for the next couple of days and asked for help, specifically for your help. Says you're trust worthy, dedicated, etcetera, etcetera, and etcetera. So, unless you prefer sleeping in ditches and eating cold canned mystery rations, I'd suggest you pull up a seat and get started."

"Don't have to ask me twice. What do you need done, Jones?"

"I need you to go ask Cook what it would take to feed the entire platoon for 30 days while traveling in the field. Tell him that whatever will be easiest to transport, for meals cooked outdoors, is what he should calculate. Make a complete list ... Oh, and Thurman, keep it quiet. Then get that list to me right away cause there'll be more stops for you. I'll get started placing orders."

Thurman took off and at the tent door, bumped straight into Rossi. Thurman grinned at Rossi, "Say, I'm sorry for being rude before but I sure was enjoying that snooze. Just got into the sack after ten days on patrol."

Hearing that exchange, Clarence called out "Hey, Rossi! You want to join this paper team, here? I could use another pair of fast feet to help gather information and you do already know the mission. Sgt. and Capt. said you'd be a big help but you took off outta here like a ruptured duck and I didn't get to ask you," Clarence asked. "What's your specialty, anyway?"

Head down, Rossi quietly replied that "I don't really have a specialty. I'm just a field grunt, looking for a way to help provide a better life for my family when I get back to Paris - Texas. But I can tear down any engine you've ever seen then rebuild it with spit and baling wire so that it runs like a spotted ass ape."

"Rossi, consider yourself an official member of team paper shuffle. But now, please take off and find whoever is in charge of the motor pool. Find out how much gasoline, oil and anything else needed to put this platoon in motion and keep it moving for as long as a month. If they think more trucks are needed, list that, too. And tanks. Find out if we need tanks. Write down everything. Remember – Keep it quiet."

Clarence set to writing up a master list:

- Food - Parker
- Transportation - Rossi
- Clothing & Laundry Supplies - Jones
- Medical – First Aid Supplies - Parker
- Ammunition – types - Rossi
- Assignments: Loading - groceries, bedding, medical

Thurman lumbered back into the tent with the cook right behind him. Cook demanded to know "Who is this yokel Private with all his busy body questions. For that matter, who the hell are you?" while Thurman held out a blank notebook at Clarence.

"Cook, you don't remember us from training at A&M? I'm Private Clarence Jones and this is Private Thurman Parker. We are both working on a project assigned by Capt. Stutz. Parker has asked for confidential information that will be critical to this platoon over the next few weeks."

Cookie, a lifelong Army man closing in on retirement replied, "Sorry boys but no, I don't recall you two specifically. I've fed thousands of hungry young upstarts in my career. So, we're picking up stakes, are we? No need to sneak around about it. It's expected. This is a war campaign. Parker, give me that notebook of yours, I'll make you a list that'll choke a mule."

They took off again - together.

Rossi came back with a list that included tanks of gasoline, oil, batteries, tires, spark plugs, fan belts, radiator caps, antifreeze, windshield wiper blades, batteries, air filters, oil filters, duct tape – miles of it, electrical tape, baling wire and flashlights.

Knowing that he better get a move on, Clarence sat down with Rossi's list and a field phone to get purchase orders in the mill so vendors could be notified. Clarence quickly learned that the ladies stationed in cities along the front lines were a very different breed than the women he chatted with while training in Texas. These women were soldiers, same as he was and were seldom in the market to buy his line of charm. His line of banter only served to irritate. Clarence had to adopt new methods immediately. But he did what he had to and got the P.O.s issued. Vendors already knew to put every field order through as a rush so the trucks and spare parts began arriving within 48 hours right along with more than a ton of groceries, dozens of pairs of wool socks, boots and khakis, soap and bleach plus medical paraphernalia. Plus shirts, dozens of khaki shirts arrived. The only surprise came when the request for bedding was denied.

Captain said the men should take the blankets from their cots. Sheets and pillows would just be an extra burden. There would seldom be a flat spot to lay them down anyway.

In less than a week, all the supplies were received, inventoried and sorted for temporary storage. Every soldier in camp had their personal stuff packed and ready to roll. On the 2nd day of January, 1917, the 97th Aggie Infantry division churned into motion, moving northward on up through Italy toward the Austrian border where they veered westward across a tip of Switzerland bound for France.

Every soldier in the 97th thought about what they would be doing if they were still at home at the start of this New Year. They would be spending it with family and friends, shaking off the after effects of their New Years Eve celebration and eating black eyed peas and cabbage with ham and cornbread. Six months ago, none of them would have dreamed nor could have imagined that they would be sleeping in the dirt some 5,000 miles from home. During the day, they marched in the road, moving into the woods toward nightfall. They burrowed into the underbrush for warmth as those thin blankets didn't help much against the cold wintry nights. Spending nights in the woods also offered a little protection from advancing enemies who tended to move at night.

By January 10, 1917, with just eight days on the move, Clarence decided he'd had about enough of this marching business so he elbowed Thurman and grunted. He veered off to the left in the general direction of the road, intending to see if he could sweet talk a ride with Cook on the transport convoy. If nothing else, maybe they'd let him stow his duffle so he would then be carrying only his rifle, ammo, canteen and some rations. In about an hour, he caught up with the Kitchen supply truck, spotted Cook and trotted to get alongside close enough to talk. "Hey, Cook! How's the ride?"

Cook glanced down at Clarence with a grimace, "Better'n walking. Want to jump on the back? You'll have to bail if we run up on Captain. He ain't much for the enlisted men loafing."

Happy for even a short lift, as the flat bed passed, Clarence made an easy leap up amongst the bags of rice and beans. So far, the company diet had been okay. Mostly starch and canned meat. But, it was keeping their guts full. This was not Cookie's first field rodeo.

A couple of comfortable hours passed with Clarence fitfully dozing, feeling a little guilty for riding when so many of his fellow soldiers suffered the cold, wet, critter-laden march bound for France. The screeching of brakes broke into his reverie and the voice of Capt. Stutz brought him to attention. At least, he was fully alert though still sitting on a 100 pound sack of potatoes when Capt. strode around back of the truck. For about 10 seconds, he just stared at Clarence then, "I think you should get down from your perch there and join your pals, Private Jones. You may need them one of these days and it would be a shame if none of them heard you holler for help."

Clarence knew what Captain was saying so he jumped off the back of the truck as quickly as he'd jumped on. Rested up, he took off into the woods, looking for Thurman or Rossi. He didn't find anyone familiar except a couple of officers from A&M boot camp days. One of the Lieutenants glanced at Clarence then, nodding to his buddy, said "Well, look who we have here. Ol' Mr. Goody-Goody Jones . . . sent back to school for extra learning. Just so he can order potatoes and rifle shells. Made him think he's too good to march with the rest of the platoon."

Clarence didn't say anything except "Sir" with a snappy salute.

The two Aggies, on horseback, rode off, leaving Clarence to consider his future. He trudged on, just out of sight in deep underbrush between the actual woods and the road. He could hear the guys up ahead since they weren't making any special effort to be quiet. After about an hour, he realized he could no longer hear the trucks on the roadway but the noise from the platoon was getting a little louder.

All of a sudden, two arms grabbed him from behind, a hand clapped over his mouth. Clarence bit down as hard as he could on that soft muscle between the thumb and the forefinger. As he bit, he stomped backward on the top of his attacker's foot. Thurman Parker let out a bellowing yell and dropped his arms from around Clarence's chest.

"What the hell was that for? Why'd you bite me, you cannibal? "

"Why'd you sneak up and grab me like that? Don't you realize that I could a shot you?"

"Sneak up? I came tromping through bushes, leaves, sticks, twigs, brambles and rocks about as quietly as a 3 legged elephant. I was making enough noise to wake the dead. It's you that could easily been killed. Boy, you need to get your head outta your drawers and pay attention to your surroundings. You stumble into a hornet's nest and you'll endanger more than just yourself. There are a couple of us guys who just might come to your aid and you'd be putting us in deep stuff, too. So, wake up and join the rest of us here in this war!!

This was a pretty stern speech from Thurman who generally was not a big talker. He sure wasn't one to offer advice or directions to another person on how they should conduct themselves. Knowing this, Clarence figured he better pay attention. At least until the platoon made it into France.

Clarence had adapted to military life better than even he had expected. And far better than anyone who knew him figured he would. Clarence knew his own shortcomings pretty well which in the long run, is actually a strong characteristic. Most people can name their strengths but when asked about their weak spots, they hesitate for a variety of reasons; embarrassment or ego. But not Charlie Clarence. He knew that he did not take direction from others well. Not that he didn't understand them; he just didn't appreciate being told that his behavior needed changing. He also resented the expectations other people seemed to have of him; the sense of responsibility those expectations always forced.

Clarence was primarily a decent human being; he just didn't like the shackles of adulthood. Burdens like a wife, a farm and five children were the very reasons he'd enlisted in the Army. And the childhood memories he continued to try to forget. Clarence knew, of course, that there was a war on and he'd probably get sent to Europe but, he had failed to grasp the enormity of that commitment. Now, these new Army buddies seemed to depend on him just like all the people back in East Texas. The thought of this could sometimes almost make him choke on his own breath.

"Well," Clarence told himself, "In for a penny, in for a pound." He had no choice now but to step up and do his part. So, with a staggering sigh, he hoisted his duffle and rifle back onto his shoulder and headed toward the voices, hoping they were his marching pals and that Thurman would not be mad any more. He sort of hoped he'd run into Rossi or even Sgt. Odell.

The sun was beginning to cast long shadows through the woods, making the trees appear menacing and evil. Clarence had been able to ignore the cold so far but now, as he realized night was creeping up on him, he felt chilled to the core. His feet were blistered, aching and stiff. He wanted nothing more than to sit down and rest. He knew that stopping was not an option, though, and he had to keep walking.

Rossi worried about the progress being made by the platoon. So far, Capt. had them stopping every night, pitching bivouac and letting Cookie fire up the big stove as if they were on a Boy Scout weekend adventure in Mobeetie, Texas.

Rossi wasn't convinced, either, that this was the way an aggressive military battle was mounted but he knew not to open his mouth. He'd heard Sgt. Odell ask Capt. whether it was wise to create all the smoke from the stove and other fires. Capt.'s reply was hot enough to keep a barracks tent warm all night. Rossi feared the platoon was moving too slow, making too much noise and leaving too big a trail.

Their march upward to France followed wooded areas, small rivers and almost dry white rock creek beds, heading toward the Sommes River. To the boys of East Texas, the land appeared to be rich enough for farming though there was little evidence of anything being grown. Nothing other than small family gardens that they stumbled into occasionally. The land lay flat, sloping toward the creeks where it then found shade and water. Some of the men wondered if the quiet, easy feeling given off by the landscape had lulled the officers into forgetting what their mission was supposed to be.

Thurman worked his way through the woods East of the platoon, staying about 100 yards off the right flank. There was one of the A&M lieutenants, Dan Berry, between him and the first column so if enemy soldiers appeared, the Aggie would draw the first round then Thurman would return fire. This commotion would give the platoon time to drop and defend. A simple but so far, untested, strategy. About the time Thurman noticed the platoon begin to slow, noise off to his left caused him to duck, drop and chamber a round. Almost at the same moment he hit the ground, he heard Clarence say,

"Kinda jumpy there, aren't you, Private? . . . Hey, just kidding, I saw you stalking the Aggies and figured I'd join you. Mind the company?" Thurman got back to his feet and replied,

"Course not. But maybe we should fan back to the left a bit for a broader view of the platoon."

In that instant, the 'crack' of a low caliber rifle startled both of them. They hit the ground in unison, Clarence facing toward the platoon which was still moving away from them; Thurman faced the opposite direction. Only a handful of soldiers looked around as though they'd heard anything. The Aggie officers never flinched and continued following the rest of the squadron.

Thurman and Clarence looked at each other, Clarence raising his head enough to glance left and right. Laying boots to helmet next to each other, Thurman looked up, too but he was facing nothing but trampled woods where they had just been. About 150 yards ahead, to the left of the platoon but close to the tree line, Clarence saw Rossi pop straight up in the air then drop back down to all fours. Clarence gave a gentle kick to Thurman's lid and whispered, "Look over there" as Rossi scrambled toward them like a scared crab.

Thurman called out, "What's up, Rossi? You practicing 'the barb wire crawl'?"

"No, Man! Didn't you hear that shot? Somebody must've seen me cleaning my rifle and figured it'd be the perfect time to take me out. Lucky I'm still alive."

"Which way did the shot come from? What'd it hit?"

"Other side the Aggie boys, I think. Hit into the dirt about 15 feet behind where I was sitting – on that log." Rossi pointed in the direction where he'd been when the shot rang out.

Thurman and Clarence got to their feet, pulled Rossi up off the ground and started walking toward where he'd pointed. But not before Clarence paused to brush all the leaves and brambles off his shirt. As they walked, Rossi nervously rambled, "We better get down. The next shot could come at any minute and here we are – big old, slow moving targets. You know, one of those Aggie Lieutenants might've fired that shot accidentally. Or, maybe just to shake me up a little. You know, I wouldn't put it past either one of those guys. They seem like pranksters. Look up there at them. Don't they seem kinda skittish now?"

"Not as much as you do," sniped Clarence. "You sure you didn't accidentally fire that round?"

"Durn your hide, Private Jones. Why would you accuse me of that?"

"No accusations," Thurman chimed in as he rattled the ever present acorn. "I wondered the same thing. No shame in an accident. It could happen to anybody."

The three of them walked on, covering the 40 yards to the log quickly. Rossi sat back down to show them what he'd been doing. Thurman stepped off about 15 more yards behind and to Rossi's left. He found a spot at the base of another tree, right at ground level, where the dirt was disturbed. There was a small spot that was clean of underbrush and bark on the tree was peeled away, leaving a small hole.

Squatting down at the spot, Thurman took his pocket knife and began to dig in the hole. It took only a couple of minutes for Thurman to dig out a spent .22 shell. Palming it, he walked back over to where Rossi and Clarence sat. Clarence was holding Rossi's rifle and talking to him quietly. Rossi seemed to be calming a little.

Just as Thurman reached them, he noticed Clarence sniff the end of the barrel. Clarence asked Rossi, "You sure you didn't accidently fire your weapon? It's nothing to be ashamed of but it does need to be reported." Clarence glanced up as Thurman handed him the shell which was U.S. Army issue – the same ones all the soldiers carried.

Their movements were not lost on Rossi. He stood up, looking between Clarence and Thurman as he said, "Okay, All right. It was me. I accidently fired the round. Thought I'd emptied the rifle when I sat down to clean it. When I pulled the hammer back, it slipped and there it went. You don't know how thankful I am that nobody was hurt. I'd be ridiculed, run out of this man's army, if any of the guys or officers found out. You won't report me, will you, Clarence?"

"Not gonna report *you*, Rossi. But I have to record the incident. Part of my sworn duty."

"But what if you hadn't seen it happen?"

"But I did see it happen."

Thurman threw in, "And I'm a witness. There could be others, too. Those Aggies just over yonder; they ain't deaf."

"It'll be the end of my military career. I'll get sent home. Be a laughing stock. I won't be able to get a job or provide for the family. Jones, are you dead certain you have to report me? I'll be your aide for the rest of this war," plead Rossi.

"Rossi, don't beg. It ain't becoming. You know what I have to do. It's not personal. Come on now, we better catch up with the platoon. Be time to pitch camp here pretty quick."

Rossi grabbed his rifle out of Clarence's hands and without another word, stalked off toward the troops, back ramrod straight with head high.

"You really gonna report Rossi?" Thurman asked.

"Course not. I will record the incident but unless some officer asks me, it'll stay in a locked bag inside my duffel until that unfortunate 'bonfire incident.' That'll show Rossi accidents can happen to anybody."

With a huge grin, Thurman grabbed Clarence around the shoulders and gave him a shake by the shirt collar. "Brother, you're okay; I don't care what anybody else says about you!"

Clarence ducked away, "Stop it! You're messing up my shirt!" But he did laugh right out loud, enjoying being treated like just one of the Guys.

Routine set in with the platoon steadily covering only about nine miles each day. Sleep, such as it was, could only be found in the woods which broke the wind a little but the bitter cold was beginning to take a toll on everyone. None of the 97th was accustomed to winter than lasted for six months at a time. They grew up with the occasional freezing night then by noon the next morning, 50 degrees. Several of the men suffered frost bite, some even losing toes or fingers. Pneumonia and dysentery claimed the lives of about a dozen soldiers. The medical support team was kept busy throughout the entire march.

But one of the biggest war diseases was homesickness. All of the soldiers suffered from it in one way or another. Men missed their wives, children and sweethearts. Some missed their mothers and families as a whole. Some even longed to see their dogs. Coping came in many forms; bragging, jokes and pranks, gambling, serious Bible study with prayer groups formed by the non-denominational chaplain who marched right along with the unit. Letter writing became a major outlet. Everyone continually foraged for paper and pencils.

Then there was Trench Art; the work of truly talented artists, using only the materials and tools found along the way. Spent artillery shells of various calibers became toy airplanes or trains, a lot of the art had a patriotic theme. Other pieces were pure whimsy. It turned out that Clarence was a skilled whittler with the pocket knife that he'd brought with him from Athens.

But the doughboys marched on, crossing into southern France by late April, 1917. A collective sigh of relief was exhaled. The unit had been traveling at the edge of enemy territory for more than three months without so much as a skirmish – if you don't count Rossi's misfire. Sadly, this feeling of relative safety was a serious error. The boys were about to be pulled into some of those battles that Sgt. Odell had warned them about way back in boot camp.

More U.S. of A. ground troops were beginning to arrive in France which contributed to Clarence and the boys' false sense of security. However, they were about to meet with vicious German resistance. It was not until June, 1917 that air support was ready to leave New York City bound for the United Kingdom. Surrounded by an armada of destroyers, the fleet made remarkable time crossing the Atlantic. They met up with British allies just off the coast of Ireland, at last making landing in France on June 30th.

Rossi continued to worry about how slowly Captain Stutz persisted in moving the platoon northeasterly toward their assigned destination. They were supposed to meet British allies along the Sommes River in the Picardie region by August 1st but at the rate they were moving, it'd be Halloween before they arrived. Rossi had kept his thoughts to himself but it was getting harder every day. And, Dad Gum It . . . his feet hurt!!!

Thurman Parker maintained an ever watchful eye as he continued to march at the right flank. He could see the mounted Aggie officers ahead and Clarence off to his left. The daily humdrum didn't bother Thurman all that much as he marched along, rattling that acorn that he *always* carried. Thurman began rattling that acorn as a young boy when his mama died. The movement of his hands seemed to sooth his mind. As he prepared to leave home for the Army, he packed a bag of them in his duffel so one would always be handy. He often gave those acorns to children as a way to put them at ease because a dried acorn with the cap still on will rattle, like a toy. Thurman enjoyed seeing children laugh and be happy, though he had no kids himself . . . yet.

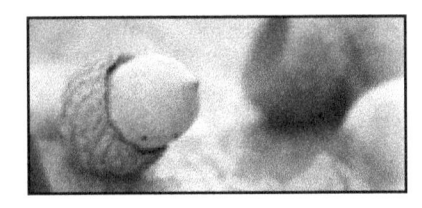

Once in a while, Rossi dropped back with a robust "Hey, Boy. How're you holdin' up?" And sometimes, Sgt. Odell appeared to check up on him. So, it made Thurman scratch his own head when he sometimes felt all down in the mouth, wishing somebody would cover his flank so he could relax a little. And, Dang it All . . . His feet were killing him!!!

Clarence protected the left flank to the best of his ability. He stayed on pace with Thurman whom he watched through the woods over to his right about 75 yards. Clarence sometimes wondered what the two of them would be able to do if an attack from the rear did happen. He wondered how much defense they and the two Aggies on horseback would offer. Clarence often wondered what this war was about and why the good old U.S. of A. was even involved. He wondered just who in thunder this Archduke Ferdinand of Austria had been to warrant getting killed then having a full blown world war fought on his behalf. He wondered what Sgt. Odell wanted him to say when he dropped back to complain about Captain Stutz's leadership skills. Sgt. was of the same mind as Rossi: They were moving way too slow and not doing near enough to hide their presence. Clarence wondered if Captain Stutz didn't realize that France wasn't exactly friendly territory just because they were an ally. France was the primary target of the German assault and with the route they were following, they were well within artillery range of the border. As if the enemy just stopped marching once they reached the border of another country.

The soldiers and officers got along okay, at least on the surface. There was obvious tension between Sgt. Odell and Capt. Stutz. But none of the soldiers realized how deep the festering feud was or what an unlikely turn it was about to take.

Slogging onward, the troops tried to keep each other's spirits up. Cookie surprised the ranks with pies one night after supper. As the platoon passed through the village of Epinal, Cookie found a bakery that still had butter for which he traded 10 pounds of flour. Cookie had hoarded flour which the French needed for bread. The bakery also had apples stored in a root cellar that they were glad to give to their American allies. The aroma of baking pies got to the guys long before anyone had a taste. No one remembered what was for supper that night but everyone remembered apple pie. Amazing how far a little sugar goes to boost morale. That pie was a topic of discussion for a month!

Clarence continued his duties as company clerk but there wasn't a lot to be done in that role at the moment. So far, he'd re-ordered some dry goods for Cookie and a few parts for the Motor Pool. Not a hostile shot had been fired so there'd been no need to restock ammunition. And as far as he was concerned, that was a fine situation.

The gang trudged on for another uneventful six weeks, slowly covering a mere 200 miles. By now, the leisurely pace was working the nerves of all the men. Even the young Aggie officers thought their advancement was not what it should be. Rookie Lieutenant, Dan Berry, was assigned to shadow the Captain. But by this time, young Berry had lost all confidence in the decisions being made by Capt. Stutz. Dan didn't think he could talk to Sgt. Odell so he singled out Clarence for advice from an 'older soldier.' Clarence was quick to point out that he was merely a private, a grunt foot soldier. Lt. Berry made it clear that he wasn't really looking for advice as much as a sounding board for an idea he had.

One evening after mess, Clarence was alone in the officer's tent ordering powdered milk and spark plugs when Lt. Berry stepped in. Instead of sitting down, he paced back and forth, wringing his hands and nervously clearing his throat. An image of Slick instantly popped into Clarence's mind, bringing on a sudden wave of homesickness. He stood, saluted Berry then said, "Anything I can help you with, Sir?"

Without preamble, Lt. Berry announced, "I'd bet you my horse, Star – the finest mare to ever volunteer for the U.S. Army – that Capt. is slow-footin' it cause he's afraid to push us into the front line. He's afraid of getting shot, just like you're afraid of getting dirty."

Clarence was taken aback and a little miffed. "I ain't *afraid* of getting dirty. I just don't much care for it."

"Broad as it is long, Jones. But listen here. I have a plan. A plan that will put ME in charge of this operation. I can handle it. I know I can, with the help of my fellow graduate, Lt. Couples and input from you old guys... You and Cookie."

"Cookie may be able to give you advice but not me. I'm not one of the 'old guys' just cause I'm a ten years older than you. I'm a rookie, fresh out of boot, same as everybody else here. I can listen to you and tell you if your idea doesn't seem to make much common sense. Otherwise, I'm a sounding board – just like that fence post you talk to sometimes. Have you talked to Sgt. Odell about your idea? Say, what IS your idea anyway?"

"No, I haven't talked to Sgt. because I'm afraid he'd tell Capt. I know Sgt. isn't a full-fledged officer and that I do actually outrank him but still . . ."

"Sgt. is a cool guy and trust me, he won't be telling Capt. anything unless you plan to kill him. Then, I think he might mention it. Hell, if you plan to kill him, I'll be forced to bring it up. I certainly hope that's not your plan."

"Course not! But I do plan to get rid of him. You know that sometimes, when we first break camp, I ride to the right of Capt. as he tools along in the Jeep. One day, we'll be just alongside when Star suddenly spooks and rears up. The driver will have to make a sharp left to keep Star from bringing her front hooves down on top of Capt. I figure he might even fall out of the Jeep. Probably suffer a few cuts and bruises - maybe a broken arm – just enough to get him shipped off to the hospital. This is where you come in, Clarence.

You'll need to make sure the medics know that Capt. is to be sent to hospital since they'll have to sign off on the paperwork. Sgt. needs to be in on the deal so he can have Rossi driving on the day of the accident. I think Rossi can handle the Jeep in an accident better than Morgan plus he knows how to keep his mouth shut. And Clarence, we need to figure out a way to keep Major Elkhart from coming up from Italy to take over command. He needs to be assured that the platoon will be in good hands if I'm in charge and that we'll make the arrival with the Allies right on time. What do you think? Are you in? Will you help?

While Clarence was bored to pieces with the daily routine of marching and sleeping on the ground, he wasn't convinced that speeding up the charge would benefit anybody. Nor did he like the idea of a commanding officer being set up for bodily harm. But, he also knew that this young officer could make his life miserable if he wanted to so his answer had to be 'just right.'

"Hmm. Sounds like to me, Lt. Berry, that you have given a lot of thought to your plan. And I do understand your frustration. Plus, I know for a fact that Sgt. Odell as well as some of the other soldiers agree with you so you have a lot of support already. And believe me; I'm as tired as anyone of what seems to be this pointless

LEAVE THE LAMP ON...

strolling across France. However, convincing the medical team to send Capt. to the hospital for what you say will be minor injuries won't be easy. Also, the number of people you plan to include on this escapade is sure to cause you some grief. You've heard the old saying, "If two people are in on a secret, one of them will tell it then that's the end of your secret." And finally, who're we trying to impress by rushing to the bivouac area? I know that the German/Austrian forces are watching us. We look like a bunch of kids at church camp. But if we turn into an efficient military machine overnight, they will get the impression that now we've become the aggressors which is bound to look suspicious and probably annoy them."

Lt. Berry listened to Clarence intently, hanging on every word, appearing to earnestly consider the input. But then, he replied, "I'm sorry it doesn't sound like you think my idea is a good one. I'm going forward with my plan regardless." All Clarence could say was that he hoped it worked out to the best for everyone.

With that, the daily ritual prevailed. Reveille sounded at 0500, Cookie served something resembling breakfast at 0600, the motor pool rolled out at 0700 with the 182 man platoon marching roadside, just in the far edge of the woods about a half mile behind.

This pattern continued for another two weeks then, one morning, right after everyone mobilized, a volley of gunfire broke out from the right flank. The first to fall was Aggie Lt. Dan Berry. He was followed by about six of the foot soldiers on right side of the platoon. Thurman was his usual 75 yards back and hadn't been hit. He dropped to the ground but didn't return fire because by the time he rolled into position, there was nobody to shoot at. In less than a minute, Clarence fell in beside him, racking a round in the slide chamber. Both men were on full alert but with no leadership in sight, it was hard to know which way to jump. So far, there had been no return fire to that first round of shots. Clarence hissed at Thurman so he'd see that he'd laid down his rifle then pulled out the small two-way Motorola radio that he carried when Rossi was on driver duty. As it happened, Rossi was traveling with the motor pool that day. Capt. Stutz was at the front of the motorized caravan and today, Rossi was driving his Jeep.

Due to Clarence's tone on the radio, Rossi didn't make any jokes. He handed the receiver to Capt. Surprised, Capt. listened to Clarence for a full 60 seconds without a word then said, "I'm on the way back to you with the medics." Handing the radio back to Rossi, he commanded, "Turn this Jeep around." He shouted back to the medical truck just behind his Jeep, "Turn it around. We've been hit. Clarence says we've got at least seven down, including Lt. Berry. I don't know why he was back there today. I don't know why you're driving today. Guess it doesn't matter."

Rossi didn't have to be told to gun it. He didn't even tell Capt. to hold on. He made a smart U-turn, bouncing down into then out of the ditch and was headed to the rear flank in under a minute flat. The medic truck immediately followed. Rossi radioed the situation to the drivers in the other trucks so everyone U-turned to follow Rossi.

In the meantime, Clarence and Thurman began crawling toward Lt. Berry as he lay beside his horse, Star. The mare was as still as Berry. Lt. had taken a bullet in his side just behind his right arm. Though there was very little bleeding, he wasn't breathing. Thurman got to him first, slapping the mare's rump. Star whinnied and raised her head then gained her footing. She wasn't hurt but had lain still until help arrived to protect her commanding officer. Clarence looked off toward where he thought the gunfire came from – no movement, no sound. He stood up, breaking into a trot toward the soldiers who were downed up along the flank. Their buddies were beginning to stand as well.

Rossi knew how far behind the motor brigade that the troops usually were so when he'd sped two miles back, he cut left, bouncing across a shallow ditch. Unfortunately, Capt. failed to maintain a solid grip and ended up on his behind in the dirt. His tail bone and his pride were both shattered. Rossi jumped out to help but Capt. waved him away, "Go on. Find Clarence. Get me details. Take the medics with you."

By this time, the medical team had arrived. A couple of them glanced at Capt. but never slowed down as they ran to keep up with Rossi. From the middle of the platoon, Rossi had watched the rear enough to know the approximate distance behind the group to look for the Lt. It only took a minute to spot the fellows gathering around Berry so the medics picked up their pace, running in that direction. Rossi spotted Thurman since he was half a head taller than most of the other guys. Thurman was looking down as Clarence tightened a tourniquet on the arm of a bleeding private. He had made the tourniquet out of his own belt. Standing up, Clarence looked around to see who else needed help. It was then he realized that medical support was there. He stepped aside as the medics took over.

Rossi bolted straight to Clarence and Thurman. "What happened?" he shouted at the same time Clarence squawked "Where's Captain?" Thurman answered, "We got shot! Where's Captain hiding?"

Rossi interjected, "Capt.'s not hiding. He forgot to hold on when I turned off the road into the woods across the ditch. He ended up on his ass in the dirt. Think his back is hurt pretty bad."

Clarence, "So where is he?"

"Still back there lying in the ditch. He wouldn't let any of the medics stop to tend to him. He said to get to the others first and see to Lt. Berry. They can get back to him later."

Thurman, "No need to rush. Not for Lt. Berry any way. But there are other men who could sure use some attention."

Dumbstruck, Rossi demanded," What are you saying?"

"I'm saying, Lt. Berry didn't make it. He took a direct hit into his right side that likely collapsed a lung and no telling what else. Hell, the fall off that horse would've been enough by itself to kill a man. But the big ol' girl sure tried to take care of him."

Clarence added, "She sure did that. Don't guess Lt. Berry's plan for today worked out quite the way he'd hoped."

Rossi flopped down to the ground, "What's wrong with you two? A soldier, a man that you ate breakfast with three hours ago, is now dead. Gone. Finished. Snuffed out by enemy fire and no one here returned a shot? Don't you find that creepy and a little bit strange? Y'all know he didn't intend to hurt anybody."

"Hey! Rossi, calm down. Nobody has anything bad to say about him. Nobody is accusing anyone of anything. But you knew Lt. Berry's plan to get rid Captain out of the way and take over the platoon. Just weird coincidence that on the day he decided to implement his scheme, a war breaks out and he is the first to get killed."

Thurman added, "Nobody returned a shot because 1) Everyone was busy finding cover; 2) No officer gave the order to return fire and 3) Lt. Couples was still on his horse and had moved between the flank back toward Berry and in the general direction of the attack. "

"Say . . . Where is Lt. Couples?" Asked Clarence. "I didn't see him when I got to you, Thurman."

Rossi, "I don't see him now, either. He couldn't just disappear. Not on that red horse he rides."

Clarence, Thurman and Rossi all stood up, turning toward the rest of the platoon. The medics were busily applying bandages and getting stretchers ready to make the trek back to the trucks. The three Privates surveyed the area as a whole. Thurman hollered, "There! Look there" as he pointed toward the front line and a nearby creek.

There was Lt. Couple's big red horse, Ginger. They all struck a trot toward the mare, slowing on approach so as not to spook her.

Ginger stood perfectly still as the boys neared, letting Rossi cradle her neck and pick up her reins. There was absolutely no sign of Lt. Couples. It looked like he'd just dismounted and walked off. Clarence stepped back to get a better view of the grass around the horse. He noticed that it was flattened out a bit to the right of the mare then trailed away a few feet before returning to normal. This faint trail led east about 20 yards then vanished as the grass thinned along rocky banks of the Sommes River. Clarence felt that Lt. Couples may have been taken prisoner but had no actual evidence to go on other than the beaten down grass trail which, he knew, wouldn't last long at all. Walking back toward the opposite tree line where the soldiers had gathered just inside the shade, Clarence began asking questions of each group of men about what they'd seen when the shots rang out. Did anybody see Berry get hit? Did anybody see which way Couples went? Did anybody see any German soldiers? Getting only negatives answers, he said to Thurman, "What do you think about this thing here?"

Thurman replied, "Likely the same thing you're thinking. Couples didn't just wander off of his own free will."

Clarence says to Rossi, "You still toting that radio thing?"

"You bet. Right here in the pack."

"Better try to get hold of Major Eckhart back in Italy then. Looks like Lt. Couples has been taken prisoner. With him missing, Lt. Berry killed, and Captain out of commission, that leaves Sgt. Odell in charge. You know they'll want an officer here . . . and frankly, so do I." Rossi took off at a trot toward the clearing to get a better airwave signal.

By this time, the most urgent medical work was finished and the team was heading back to the trucks. There were only two soldiers injured seriously enough to be carried out on stretchers. But the 10 or 12 others with shrapnel hits would be unfit for duty for a while so they were also on the way to the trucks. Clarence and Thurman stayed behind to try and restore a little order to the soldiers, to mind the flank and keep alert for additional pot shots.

When the group got back to the trucks, Capt. Stutz was still laying in the same exact spot where he landed when he fell out of the Jeep. He had taken on a gray, ashy color and his breathing was shallow. One of the corpsmen checked his vitals and determined that his heart and pulse were good though his blood pressure was a bit low. This was likely due to pain, shock and fear. Fear because, after all, the Captain had been left alone, in enemy territory, injured and defenseless against anybody who might happen along. When the medics attempted to roll Capt. onto a stretcher, he made it abundantly clear that he was not happy with that plan. One of the almost docs glanced at Rossi and mumbled "could be a broken back."

Rossi stepped forward and gave Capt. Stutz an update on the situation; Lt. Berry killed, Lt. Couples missing, two soldiers seriously injured. 12 others caught enough shrapnel to be off duty for a while. No return fire and no additional enemy fire. Then, Rossi dropped the real bomb. "Sir, I'm about to radio Major Eckhart with an update. We'll need some leadership here on the ground, other than Sgt. Odell, that is. Just until you get back on your feet."

Rossi expected Capt. to explode at the idea of involving Major Eckhart. Instead, Capt. said, "That's likely the best move to make. Tell him to consider your call as my official incident report. Where are Privates Jones and Parker?"

"They stayed back with the fellows to help keep an eye out in case of another ambush."

"Tell them I appreciate them and if anything should happen, they are to put out a 'hold your ground' order with an immediate return fire. We'll talk about strategy tonight after everyone is back at bivouac and after Major is onboard. Medics, let's roll."

Rossi popped a snappy salute as Captain was loaded into a truck. Then, he radioed Major Eckhart with the bad news. Eckhart was surprisingly calm, asking only about casualties and location.

Rossi answered as best he could then signed off. He told a trembling Morgan to drive the Jeep back to camp then he gave Capt. the details from Major and took off back toward Clarence and Thurman. He found them, gathered together with the rest of the platoon, squatted down on their heels the way countrymen do. Rossi swore later than it looked like they were having prayer meeting.

As Rossi approached, Clarence stood then raised his hat in the air, same as he did back in basic, and everyone quieted down. "What's the word, Rossi?"

"Captain is going to be laid up for a while. Medic isn't sure yet but thinks his back could be broken. Major Eckhart was surprisingly calm. He said to tell you and Parker that he appreciates your effort in this situation and that if anything else happens, you should give the order to 'Hold your ground with an immediate return fire.' There'll be strategy discussion tonight back at camp once Major arrives and passes along what he wants us all to do."

Thurman was just walking around, leading Ginger so Clarence climbed up on her for better visibility then waved his hat again before speaking up, "Okay y'all. Listen up.

We've got orders from the Major in case of another attack. It'll be an immediate "Hold your ground with return fire." This is from the Major, not me even though if this should happen, either Thurman or I will yell it out. If we find ourselves in such a situation, we'll fire back but keep moving forward. Always move forward. Pass the word along.

As for the rest of the day, I think we should move west closer toward the road so we can at least try to hear the trucks until we reach camp for the night. Is everybody good with that approach?"

Mumbled agreement was the only response until a question rang out, "What about Lt. Couples? Shouldn't we try to find him?"

This time, Thurman spoke up, "We'll get more orders tonight from Major. He may want some of us to go out on a search party. He may even bring some guys who're trained in reconnaissance but for now, we'll follow the instructions that Clarence passed along. We're not abandoning Couples; we're just doing what's best for the whole platoon first."

"Fall in. Leads, remember, we'll march forward left."

With no disagreement, the men gathered their packs and weapons then fell into rough order to restart their march. By now, it was close to noon so many of the guys were walking along eating rations, seemingly oblivious to their surroundings. Progress back toward the road was slow but eventually, it was visible through the woods. The trucks were long out of sight however so; changing direction to direct west, the 97th platoon cleared the woods and proceeded forward on the road, in full view of anybody who might be watching.

The rest of the day passed quietly and by late afternoon, the platoon caught up with the motorcade back at camp. Captain Stutz was medicated and sleeping in a make-shift hospital tent. Cookie was just beginning to get the evening meal ready and the men were lazing about, quietly rehashing the day's events as dusk hurried toward dark.

Clarence, Thurman and Rossi and some of the other men were setting up the mess tent when a Jeep came bouncing into camp and Major Eckhart hopped out. As soon as the Jeep's engine noise faded, Sgt. Odell looking shocked boomed out, "Fall in, men."

A scramble to order ensued but after about five minutes, all the men stood at parade rest next to the partially finished mess tent, facing Major. Even Cookie came out to hear this speech.

"Men, you've suffered a loss today. Nobody has to tell you this. You've seen your first small skirmish and gotten a taste of war. You've suffered a defeat and learned what

LEAVE THE LAMP ON...

it means to move on. This does not mean you're forgetting Lt. Berry or abandoning Lt. Couples. In fact, tomorrow, a search party will set out to follow the trail spotted this morning by Private Jones. The team will be led by a Sgt. Taylor who will arrive a little later this evening. Taylor is specially trained in surveillance and espionage. Privates Jones, Rossi and Parker will be assigned to the team as well. As for right now, Cookie, what's for supper?"

"The usual, Sir. Mystery meat, gravy, taters and baby asparagus – locally grown."

"Still raiding abandoned fields, are you, Cookie?" joked the Major.

"From time to time, just to help balance the boys' diet," said Cookie.

"Nobody's complaining. As soon as the tent is up and supper is ready, let's eat! I've been missing Cookie's meals!"

Clarence, Thurman, Rossi and the boys fell back to raising the tent. When finished, they gave thumbs up to Major and Cookie then stood aside while all the men filed in to get trays. As sorry as they were about losing buddies, it wasn't going to prevent anyone from enjoying one of Cookie's creative evening suppers.

About halfway through the meal, the distant rumble of an approaching truck could be heard. Everyone was on full alert and poised for battle by the time the truck rolled into camp. Not only was it a U.S. Army truck, it was towing a horse trailer as well. Major and Sgt. Odell stood to go out and meet the arriving search team leader. A silence fell in the tent as the men stopped eating and stared as Major scurried back into the tent to make the introductions.

Major Elkhart did not have to call for attention when he boomed out, "Everyone, this here is Master Sgt. Helen Taylor. She will be leading the group searching for Lt. Couples. She is eager to get underway tomorrow so tonight will be an early 'lights out.' Cookie will have breakfast ready at 0500 for the team. Everyone else will be ready to roll out at 0600. Listen up now."

Six foot tall M/Sgt. Helen Taylor spoke with a strong New England accent that would make you want to go deep sea fishing without a boat. She had really big front teeth, and freckles that you could use to play connect the dots. "I realize you all are shocked and many of you will think that only fools would be a party to following me in this effort. Let me assure you that this is not my first search mission. It won't be my first *successful* mission. It won't be the first time men will try to undermine me. The two soldiers that are here from HQ for this mission are all search & rescue specialists. I'm also told that Privates Powell, Rossi and Jones will be participating due to their knowledge of the incident as well as the local terrain. With all those combined skills, we'll make short work of this mission. See you boys here in the morning."

Major spoke up, "Jones, Parker, Rossi, meet us in the officers tent now. Thank you."

M/Sgt. Taylor turned on her heel and left the mess tent with Major. As soon as Clarence, Thurman and Rossi got their jaws off their chests and closed their mouths, they headed out toward the Officers tent at next thing to a trot.

Assembled in the Officers tent were Major Eckhart, Sgt. Odell, M/Sgt. Taylor, Cookie and the three Privates plus the two young men who accompanied Taylor. She took the floor right off with, "Let's be brief. It's going to be a short night for everybody. Cookie, can you have some field chow ready for us by 0500? Enough to last a couple of days?"

"No problem there, Ma'am. It may not be French but it'll keep body and soul together."

Addressing the privates who were waiting rigidly behind Cookie, Taylor said, "Stand down, boys. We have a hard job to do, in difficult conditions so there'll be no formalities. We'll meet at 0500 to enjoy some of Cookies' coffee and biscuits. Be ready to ride at 0530. And I do mean ride. Our horses are in the trailer along with an extra that I figured might be needed. I understand that Lts. Berry and Couples mares are here. You should bring them. You all decide who rides what. Pack light men, we'll be moving quickly. Good night, all." And with that, she strode out of the Officers command center and off to a hastily constructed single tent.

For a full 60 seconds, Major, Cookie, Sgt. and the boys all sat, staring at the tent flap, holding their breath. Finally, Clarence gathered his wits and said, "Better step lively men. Looks like we're about to be put to the test."

Thurman, "By the way, Rossi are you much of a horseman? We know that Ginger and Star are gentle as lambs but the horse they're bringing in is a wild card. Who wants to take it?"

While Rossi looked at his boots, Clarence spoke up to say, "I'll take it. I'm a little bit of a wild card myself, according to some folks."

"Settled," declared Thurman. "Let's go catch some shut eye. 0500 will be here before you know it." He led the group out of the officers tent with an acorn rattle and a quick step.

Though the day had seemed to last forever, presenting greater trauma than any of the fellows had ever seen in their mostly young lives, sleep did not come easy for any of the three Privates. Thurman lay near a tree trunk thinking about riding a horse for two days, something he had not done since he was a boy and wasn't exactly excited to do again. Rossi lay next to the mess tent worrying that he might oversleep and embarrass his buddies by not being ready to roll out on time. Thurman and Rossi both felt cold and slightly soggy, as usual.

Before bunking down, Clarence went to check on Ginger who seemed to be a little skittish though she had lain down. He thought she might be missing Lt. Couples and maybe sensing the concern everyone felt. Not knowing what happened to Lt. Couples was worse than the outright loss of Lt. Berry. Clarence lay down next to Ginger and, as he draped an arm across her neck, wondered who was comforting whom. That's how he finally dozed off.

Long before the camp bugler sounded Reveille at 0500, Sgt. Taylor had made sure her team was up and prepared, checked on her own horse and the spare then made sure coffee was hot and ready. She also inspected the bags of rations Cookie had gotten together for the mission.

Cookie didn't much care for the tall, loud, pushy woman.

Clarence and Thurman both woke, listening to the hum of activity in the still dark camp. To Clarence's dismay, there was no source of water nearby so it would be another day of grit and sand. He walked over to Rossi, still rolled up in his blanket, asleep, and kicked the bottom of his boot. This elicited a mumbled, grumpy "What? It's still dark. Go away." Then he rolled over and went back to snoring.

Thurman joined Clarence in kicking Rossi until they got him fully awake though no less grumpy. "Get up. Breakfast is ready and the coffee's on." Clarence turned and headed toward mess with Thurman right beside him.

"I didn't take that boy to raise even if I do have two step-daughters nearly as old as he is."

Rossi stood, feeling a little sorry for himself but really couldn't figure why. He decided he was lucky to be included in the search party. The change would bring a little excitement to the days and give him something new to write home to his Mama about. So, rubbing his dark hair into what he hoped appeared order, he hustled, buttoning his shirt and lacing up his boots then ran to catch Clarence and Thurman. The three men went into mess together, finding M/Sgt. Taylor, Sgt. Odell, Cookie and the men from HQ gathered at one table so they joined the group just in time to hear Taylor say,

"We'll be back by dark, day after tomorrow – possibly before depending on what we find. We'll follow the road south about eight miles then veer southeast through the woods to the point of the assumed abduction. After searching the terrain, we'll wing it from there."

Turning to face the Privates, "You boys decide who's riding which mare?"

Clarence responded, "Yes, Ma'am. Rossi is riding Star and Thurman is taking Ginger. I'll try out the loaner pony."

"Excellent choice. Cookie, got our traveling grub ready?"

"Yes,'m. Six sets, stacked right behind us. Not exactly iron rations but close." Cookie wondered why she asked since she'd already inspected each kit.

"Fine, then. I don't see any reason to malinger. Pick out a grub sack and let's get after it, boys."

All the horses were saddled and tied to the bumper of a Jeep, patiently waiting. Thurman went straight to Ginger and slid up into the saddle. Clarence waited for one of the HQ fellows to single out his ride then he mounted up. While everyone else was getting adjusted, Rossi was dancing around all up under Star's neck. Clarence looked back, watching him for a minute then said, "C'mon Rossi, you're holding up the train. You said you know how to ride. Did you mean a horse or a pasture gate?"

"I'm just trying to get to know her. Don't want to spook her. Same thing you did yesterday after the, um, incident."

Without another word, Clarence faced forward and rode off. M/Sgt. Taylor glanced back and with no regard for Rossi's lagging, gave the command, "Off we go fellows. We're burning daylight." No one dared mention that it was actually still quite dark.

Taking the lead at once, she led her team of five soldiers at a brisk pace down the road toward the wooded area where yesterday's attack occurred. After about three miles, she slowed to a walk dropping back just enough so Rossi could hear her, "Get up here, young man and show me where to head into the woods. By the way, what is your name?"

"Rossi, ma'am. Alfio Rossi but everybody calls me just 'Rossi'" – I think you can see why. We're almost to the area where I lost Captain out of the Jeep. I'm awful sorry about that. Hope it doesn't get me court martialed and sent home in disgrace. From there, we headed southeast on foot."

"Thanks, 'Just Rossi'…Would you stay up here toward the front with me so I can get your input from time to time?"

Rossi puffed up to his full 5'3" and glanced back to see if Clarence had heard the conversation. He was instantly deflated when he saw Clarence and Thurman both grinning at him.

The group rode on another couple of miles when the Jeep mishap spot became visible to one and all. Rossi called out, "There! There's the spot. I see it." Not only had the Jeep incident left a scar, the medical trucks had cut a sizeable path across the bar ditch and up to the edge of the woods where they were left when the team progressed on foot.

"Thank you, Rossi. Good eye," answered M/Sgt. Taylor amid the muffled chuckles of the group. "Let's proceed to the area where Jones and Parker were when the ambush occurred. From there, we'll break, stake the horses and walk on in."

Riding through the low hanging limbs and underbrush slowed them a bit but they were easily able to follow the path taken by the medics. When they reached the clearing, Clarence spoke up,

"Sgt., there at the far tree line is where Thurman and I were yesterday morning when the shots were fired. I saw Lt. Berry slump but didn't see the exact direction that the attack came from. Thurman, you catch sight of any smoke or movement?

"Not a bit, I saw Lt. Berry fall just as Lt. Couples turned Ginger toward him. Then, we focused on the troops assembling to return fire but they realized Couples was directly in their line of fire so nobody fired a shot."

Neither Clarence nor Thurman mentioned that the soldiers had pretty much frozen in place or that none of them really thought of shooting back.

"Thurman and I dropped and took aim in the general direction since we were farther back but there was nothing to shoot at. Not a sign of anybody, no movement in the brush, nothing. It was quiet as a saloon on Election Day. Everybody waited about five minutes. Then, I noticed that Lt. Berry hadn't moved and that Ginger was grazing without Lt. Couples. There isn't much else to tell. Nobody saw anything. He just vanished, it seems. Rossi, Parker and I followed a shallow trail to the creek bank but there was nothing to be seen."

Taylor dismounted and waved everyone else to do the same. With all the ponies secured, she headed out toward the open area where the platoon had been camped. The grass which had been ankle deep was still worried flat from the 180 or so men and the horses that had bivouacked there the day before. M/Sgt. Taylor and the men from HQ went to one corner of the area, spread arms' length apart then began a slow methodical search on foot. Clarence, Rossi and Thurman watched this procedure with great interest and some confusion, wondering what they might be looking for.

"Ah ha! Here we go," cried Taylor as she bent down and pulled something up from the dirt at her feet. She'd found a spent shell. Pocketing the casing, she pulled the guys in closer then noticed the three Privates just watching from a few yards back. "Jones, you guys head on over toward the creek bank. Look for anything out of place. Try not to trample on the area. Yell out if you find anything."

As ordered, the three guys took off over to the creek where they'd last seen signs of a struggle, possibly put up by Couples. At least, they assumed that to be the case. The scene had not changed in the last 24 hours. There was a shallow trail at a right angle to the flat, muddy creek bank that veered into the water. Clarence was able to tell that quite a battle had been waged by the displacement of rocks and sticks at water's edge. He stepped around the area, crossing into the trickling creek over to the opposite bank. The clear, sparkling water was so shallow, there should've been a trail all the way through if Couples had continued to struggle. Clarence found nothing in the creek bed, so he looked around about 30 yards in both directions but found no sign of an exit from the stream.

A bit puzzled, Clarence looked up to see Thurman and Rossi about 50 yards downstream but back on the opposite side. They were peering intently at the ground so Clarence crossed back and joined them.

They'd found another spot that showed signs of a fight. Using the method that Taylor employed, Clarence had Thurman and Rossi join him, side by side to slowly inspect the area leading along and away from the creek then back toward the bivouac area. They'd just started searching when Rossi spotted a small shiny object in the low brush. Picking it up, he realized it was the Lt's uniform collar bar. Showing it to Clarence and Thurman, they continued their search and shortly discovered a wool US Army cap with insignia matching the bar just found. Clarence decided they'd better let Sgt. Taylor know what they just turned up.

Clarence had an eerie feeling about this situation so, even though he could see the Sgt. across the clearing, he didn't yell out for her. He even motioned to Rossi and Thurman to keep quiet and to follow him. Once out into the open, he broke into a trot, waving his arms to get Sgt.'s attention. She waved them to go around behind her group, to walk only on the area they'd already searched. Reaching the HQ team, Clarence handed her the cap and the insignia bar. She ordered everyone into the trees behind them for a 'quick think.'

LEAVE THE LAMP ON...

Judging from the sun, it was just about high noon so the men began breaking out some of the rations that Cookie packed for them. Taylor barked out, "All right, Clarence. What did you all see at the creek?"

"It seems as though a pretty good scuffle took place on this side of the creek then progressed into the water. Thurman and Rossi found where the fight appeared to move back to this side. It looks like a body was dragged out of the water onto the bank. We found the Lieutenant's bars on this side close to the creek then his cap about 40 feet farther back on this side."

"Thoughts? Conclusions?"

"None yet. What has your team found?"

"Nothing but one spent shell. Hard to tell the caliber. But for sure was not made in the U.S."

Rossi quickly spoke up, "I think Lt. Couples escaped from the German soldiers and ran into the woods. He would know to head north and to stay away from the road."

Sgt. Taylor responded with, "Thanks, Rossi. I think you may be on to something there. I'm not sure that I think he escaped though. I think he may be being used as a ploy. Fellows, what say we go get the horses then ride back toward the platoon for an hour or so then move into the woods for the night?" She posed it as a question but the guys all knew it was really an order.

After retrieving the horses and getting underway, M/Sgt. Taylor dropped back beside Clarence, "What say you, Jones? Thoughts on the ploy idea?"

"Not really sure what I think. But something sure seems off kilter about this deal. Doesn't seem right that Lt. Couples would be able to fight his way free from a group of armed soldiers – I don't care if he *is* an A&M trained officer. It also doesn't seem to add up that he'd be set scot free, either. It's beginning to smell like a setup or trap of some kind."

"Agreed. I'm afraid the Germans may be pushing the Lt. into use as a decoy. Wonder if we're now in behind them? Maybe it's time to get Rossi on the radio with Major Eckhart to get some help here. What do you think about this? Let's go ahead and have Rossi update Major but let's move on up through the woods toward platoon camp. If we're right, maybe we can get him back," commented Sgt. Taylor.

Clarence replied, "Sorry to disagree. There's no need to use Lt. Couples as a 'decoy' of any kind. It's not as though the platoon has been sneaking northward. We've all but sent invitations to a parade as we moved. The lack of urgency and sense of professional leadership has lead to serious dispute between the officers,

67

non-coms and even some of the soldiers. Having Rossi contact Major is probably a good idea but I'd suggest we rejoin the platoon as soon as possible and proceed with the original plan of meeting the Allies in the Picardie region – wherever that is. There's where we should begin digging trenches. I think war is about to break out for real."

"So, you don't think we should try to recapture Couples while we're out here?"

"No, I do not. I don't think they've killed him or we'd have found him. I think we should hustle on back to camp, give this some serious, logical thought and bounce some ideas off Major. If Couples has God on his side, he'll be fine until we can fetch him back."

"Jones, you surprise me. I wouldn't have thought you to be a God fearing man."

"I'm not a God fearing man. I'm a God trusting man." With that, Clarence walked away, leaving M/Sgt. Helen Taylor staring at his back.

Clarence reached Thurman and Rossi as they watered Star and Ginger. He told Rossi, "Get that radio out and get Major on the line. I need to talk to him, please."

Thurman had heard every word of the exchange so he quietly asked Clarence, "You telling him about Taylor's decoy idea?"

Never subtle, Clarence answered in full voice, "No, I'm not going to have Rossi tell Major that Lt. Couples is being used as a decoy because I don't believe that to be the case."

Sgt. Taylor stood up to her full height of over six feet, straightened her broad shoulders, set her thin lips into a flat line and stomped across the clearing to go face to face with Clarence. Glaring down her lengthy nose at him, "Seems you have forgotten who you're talking to, Private."

"No, ma'am. I know exactly who I'm talking to. A wanna be officer who has been assigned a duty that nobody else would take. Nobody else would take it because it is an impossible to win detail. No way you're finding Couples – never mind rescuing him. Obviously the krauts that took him have a full day head start and a plan. They are not flying by the seat of their pants. Now, you can be all mad if you want. Shoot, you can have me court martialed if you want. Wonder what rank is lower than a buck private? ... But I'm not making a call that will set up you, your men AND us into a sure fire death trap. Now what I will do is this; I'll ask Rossi to call the major with an update and ask for some orders. Personally, I think he should have the guys get ready to roll out and be ready to start digging trenches. Like I already told you, I think this war is close."

With that, Private Clarence Jones saluted Sgt. Helen Taylor then turned toward Rossi and Thurman. "Rossi, get that squawk box fired up and connect me to the Major if you would."

Taylor stood, stunned speechless, staring at Clarence as he took charge of her project. She was not used to being challenged by underlings and certainly not accustomed to being told she was wrong. But, though her methods might be troublesome, her main concern was that she feared he might be right – about the war being close. And that there really was nothing they could do to locate Couples right away. She was also aggravated because it was beginning to appear that she was about to be outwitted for the first time ever – by a Private, no less! So, she went back to her two HQ assigned soldiers and told them they were waiting for further instructions from the Major.

Rossi leapt into motion, cranking up the battery for the field radio then went through the steps to get the Major, handing the two pound receiver to Clarence.

"Sir, Private Jones here. I wanted to give you an update and ask for direction."

"Private, where is Sgt. Taylor?"

"Nearby, Sir. We've had a difference of opinion, you might say. So I'm calling from this limb I'm standing out on."

"We'll discuss protocol later, Private. What are the findings?"

"A scuffed up path from about where Lt. Couple fell from Ginger that goes to the creek then into the shallow water. It looks like the scuffle continued into the creek for a bit then moved back to the west side near where it started. We found a collar bar there. There is another disturbance back on the same side of the creek but about 20 feet down. Rossi found a uniform cap over there with a Lt. bar, probably Couples. One of Taylor's men found a spent German shell a good 75 yards across camp towards the west woods. Sgt.'s team has scoured the field where the platoon was camped when the skirmish happened but found nothing else. That's as much 'hard evidence' as we have. Anything else is speculation."

"What do you think, Jones?"

"Looks like a set up for the whole platoon. The Germans could have easily done a lot more damage to us than they did. It's as though the skirmish was deliberately light. Now, they've got some of us off on this wild goose chase, you're distracted and the platoon is stationary, creating a sitting target. But, I think the real intent was just to rattle us which they've accomplished. They want to follow us to where we meet up with the Allies for the real campaign. And I think that's about enough for this air wave radio."

"Jones, tell M/Sgt. Taylor to call me then she'll tell you and the team to get on back to camp today. And, Private . . . Thank you."

"You're welcome, Sir. See y'all about suppertime."

Clarence handed the radio back to Rossi who had been hovering around like a bee looking for honey. "Keep it out and cranked up. Taylor will need it in a few minutes. She has to talk to the Major, too."

Rossi stared at Clarence, puzzled and annoyed, "Well, why didn't you just hand her the radio when you were done talking?"

Clarence didn't answer, just cleared his throat and rolled his eyes. "Just do it."

Rossi sat down to check the battery pack for the radio while Clarence strolled over to where Sgt. Taylor was pretending to inspect her horse's hooves. "Ma'am, Major would like for you to give him a call right away please." She straightened up, stretched her back then, without a word, headed toward Rossi.

Rossi saw her approach and thought she was not the most attractive of females; but then, he considered that his exposure to beautiful women had been pretty limited to movie stars like Ingrid Bergman so it could be that Sgt. Taylor was pretty and he just didn't have much for comparison.

When M/Sgt. Taylor got close enough to yell without scaring the ponies or the guys (or alarming the enemy that she was quite sure were lurking in the woods beyond the creek), she boomed in her nasal New Englander voice, "Rossi, get the Ma-jah for me." Rossi handed her the receiver, set the battery pack on the ground then beat a hasty retreat toward Thurman.

Watching the exchange, Thurman smothered a chuckle as Rossi approached, shaking his head. They both turned to see where Clarence had wandered off to. They spotted him over in the shade picking leaves and dusting lint off his shirt. Clarence never worried about spots on his pants or shoes but he was a stickler about his shirts. This outdoor living was getting on his nerves, badly.

After dropping the receiver on the ground, Sgt. Taylor went straight to her horse and in one smooth motion, stepped into the stirrup and swung into the saddle. From that perch, she boomed, "Attention, All! Let's ride! And be quick about. I've told Major that we'd be back to camp by dark since there is nothing more to be done here and the trail seems cold." Without a moments' hesitation, she gave her pony a little incentive and off they went toward the road.

The rest of her team let a few minutes tick by while they secured any belongings they'd unpacked and took off after her. Clarence, Thurman and Rossi followed last, keeping an eye out for anything strange. After a solid two hours ride, Sgt. waved for everyone to move back into the edge of the woods as she'd spotted a creek which would be good for watering the horses. The group spent about 10 minutes there, resting the horses and their own behinds.

With no further conversation and no delays, the empty handed search party arrived back at bivouac just after evening mess began. Sgt. Taylor dismounted first, handing her reins to one of her accompanying soldiers then hit a stride toward the mess tent. Clarence, Thurman and Rossi rode on toward the livery 'barn' to unsaddle, rub down, water and feed their horses. The rest of the visiting soldiers followed them, leading the Sgt's mare. When all the ponies were sufficiently tended, the fellows headed back to the mess tent for their own supper.

As soon as Clarence entered the tent, the heady aromas of Cookie's skills hit him and he realized he was starving. At the same time, he grabbed a tray, Major spied him and boomed, "Jones, get over here."

Clarence turned to face him then threw a formal, very precise, salute. Once he finished filling his tray, he went to the Major's table. He mentally noted that the Sgt. Taylor was nowhere to be seen.

"You ignoring a direct command, Private?" the Major asked.

"No, Sir. Here I am. I just needed to get some grub while it's there. Cookie doesn't hold leftovers for anybody and I'm really hungry. How can I help, Sir?

"You said we needed to get off the air radio. What's on your mind, Jones"?

"I think we're heading into a real battle. I think the little scuffle was something of a warning. The 97th has been strolling across France like we're on the way to a church picnic. No doubt, the Germans and Austrians have been watching us for weeks. They're probably bored and want to speed us up. At any rate, I think we need to hustle to try and reach the meeting point ahead of schedule then set to digging some serious trenches because I'm afraid it's about to get ugly up along the north Sommes River.

"No doubt you're right, Private. There's been major fighting going on there already with the British and French allies suffering thousands of casualties. I need to radio ahead to find out where the Royals are that we're joining. I'd rather arrive a couple of days behind them – let them get a head start on those trenches! Now, you fellows eat up and get some rest. You and your two cohorts come see me in the morning, 0800."

"By the way," Clarence asked, "has Sgt. Taylor already retired for the evening?"

"You might say that. Leave it alone, Jones."

After eating a couple of helpings of brown meat, gravy and rice, Clarence and Thurman declared themselves full as ticks and ready to hit the hay. But Rossi stalled with, "Wait up. I'm not done yet" as he headed back for a third tray full. Thurman, watching him, remarked, "That boy must have a tapeworm." It took Rossi only about five minutes to clean off his tray again and declare that he was also ready to go to bed.

Thurman joked to Clarence, "Rossi can rock himself to sleep. All he needs to do is turnover on his gut." Clarence guffawed over that joke as Rossi huffed off and led the way out of the mess tent and off to his cot.

The boys passed a peaceful night, snoring soundly on their cots, fully aware that very soon, they'd all be sleeping in ditches along some river in a land where nobody speaks their language and dodging bullets for a cause they didn't understand.

0500 rolled around quickly with the dreaded company bugler announcing breakfast. Clarence didn't see any need to rush since they weren't to meet with Major for three more hours. Thurman was of the same mind but Rossi jumped up, eager to get to morning mess. An hour later, Rossi was back, yelling, "Get up, you two old goats. Get up and get dressed. Major was at chow and had decided he wants us at 0700 so you're going to need to shake leg."

Thurman rolled over, opened one eye and said, "You better not be joking, kid, if you want to live to see another meal."

"I'm not joking. Major said to get y'all on your feet and to be there, spit shined by 0700.

With a sigh, Thurman hit the floor, grabbing the khakis off the locker at the foot of his bedroll. Rossi piped up, "Major said to get shined." Thurman just growled.

Clarence, however, grabbed his duffel and pulled out a clean shirt which was wrinkled from being crammed into that lumpy bag for the last couple of months. He shook it out then took it with him as he headed to the shower tent. Rossi looked at Thurman, "What's he going to do? Wash it?"

"No idea but you can bet, Jones will be as crisp as a new dollar bill."

20 minutes later, the guys were headed to the mess tent for breakfast. As expected, Clarence's shirt looked freshly ironed. Thurman just smirked but Rossi gawked, "HOW do you do that, Jones? That shirt looks like it's just been ironed!"

"Well, it's not starched properly like Emily would do it," Clarence grumbled. "but it'll have to do. Thurman and I need to hustle now and get some of those dehydrated eggs. You ate already, right?"

"Yes, but only a little. I think I'll get some more of them eggs, they're not half bad."

Both Clarence and Thurman burst into gales of laughter. Rossi, "What?! What's so funny?"

After a quick breakfast of more mystery meat, powdered milk gravy, dehydrated eggs and chicory root coffee, the trio was ready to meet with the Major right on schedule at 0700. Clarence was ready to get on with whatever Major had in store for them. "Y'all sure you don't want to go put on some fresh clothes? You both are a little rank."

Thurman shot back, "No worse than we'll all be by the end of this war."

Clarence shook his head, "Suit yourselves. But would you mind walking downwind from me?" With that, he headed toward the Major's field office so Thurman and Rossi stuck right beside him, for joking aggravation, as much as anything.

Major was deep in conversation with M/Sgt. Helen Taylor but stopped short when he caught a glimpse of the three Privates.

"Come on in here, fellows," he blustered. "Sgt. here was telling me what fine soldiers you three are." The major glanced at Taylor then fiddled with some papers on his desk. She said nothing and never moved a muscle.

Rossi beamed, Thurman remained stoic and Clarence smirked because he knew good and well that no such conversation had taken place.

"Major, what do you need us to do this morning, Sir?"

"Join the rest of the platoon. We're spending today getting ready to roll out tonight, after supper, at nightfall, heading on to the meeting point. I decided to follow your suggestion after all and get a head start on the trenches. The British Allies are due before the end of the month so we'll have about a week's jump on them. I think it will serve us all well. Go see if you can help Cookie out then check with the motor pool. That should keep you three busy for awhile. See you at noon mess."

Rossi blushed as he called out, "See y'all later, brothers" then struck a trot straight to the motor pool.

Thurman and Clarence headed to the mess tent to check on Cookie. They both realized what an ordeal that Cookie would be going through with preparing a noon meal for 180+ men. Then turning around and feeding them supper and having to get packed up and ready to travel as soon as the pots were cleaned up.

Stepping into the mess tent, Clarence suddenly realized how much he missed home. He might get annoyed with Emily and her rigid routines but she sure knew how to set a fine meal on the table. And, she might be stern in her speech and demanding in her manner but she did love her children though she rarely let it show.

And, damn, he missed the kids, especially little Bill so much it made his stomach hurt. Way more than he'd ever thought he would. Suddenly, that old life didn't seem like the burden it used to. He decided that he would make sure he convinced Emily to let him come back home after the war, no matter how long or what it took. Then it dawned on Clarence that maybe he should write to her, tell her about everything that had gone on and what was on the horizon.

With that thought in mind, Clarence found Thurman in the kitchen with Cookie. As of right that moment, all Cookie wanted them to do was fall in and help with lunch.

"We'll pack up as much as possible after you boys eat then tonight, once supper is finished, we'll work like fools to be ready to roll. Anything that isn't done, well, it'll get tossed on top of the stuff already in the truck. If you two are half as smart as the Major thinks, you'll stick close so when we roll, you can hop on one of the 'mess' trucks. It'll sure beat walking the rest of the trip. Say, where's your little buddy?"

"He's helping over with the motor pool so he'll have a ride, for sure."

"Okay, then. Get the trays and cups set out along with the forks, knives and spoons. We still have salt 'n pepper so get that out. Then you better go get your own gear packed up so once we eat tonight, you'll be ready to fall in here loading up."

Thurman and Clarence both saluted Cookie then took off to the tent. Cookie laughed as he watched them strike a trot. Then, he stepped outside to take a deep breath of the crisp autumn air. It felt good, cooling but not yet cold. As far as Cookie was concerned, it was just about right. Autumn in France reminded him of the same time of year in the hills of Eastern Tennessee where the Fall air would wrap you in a hug so fragrant, you'd swear it was sprinkled with Grandma's baby powder. Cookie, given name Earl Ledbetter, was ready to hang up his Army knives and retire. He was excited about going home to cook for his wife, Esther. She'd stood by him for more than 30 years while he served Uncle Sam. Soon, it would be her turn.

After a couple of slow deep breaths, Cookie thought, "Them beans ain't gonna stir themselves" so he ducked back into the tent to be ready to feed his always hungry boys then tear down his kitchen and hit the road. He decided that tonight's mess would be K rations so there would be precious little to clean up.

Clarence's gear stowed quickly because he was always kept his trunk inspection ready. He went back to the Majors office to ask for some writing paper and a pen. With correspondence supplies secured, he found a quiet spot in the mess tent and began his first ever letter to Emily.

September 17, 1918…… close to the Sommes River in France

"*Dearest Emily, I do hope you read this before burning it so you'll know how sorry I am for hurting you and the kids and how much I've changed. You were right when you said I joined to get away. But what you didn't understand – and I didn't, either, then – is that I wasn't trying to get away from you . . . or the children. I wanted to be somewhere, no make that, somebody that mattered. I've always known how strong you are, that you didn't truly need me for anything. I also never knew for sure if you even loved me. Oh, I knew you cared about me, in your way. But I never felt as though you were 'in love' with me. I guess you used that up with your first husband. Dang, Em, you've been through so much. It breaks my heart for the hurt you've had to bear. Yet you just keep pluggin' along. I guess the real truth in life is that there is no other choice. Is that why you keep going? Could it be cause you love your children – and maybe me, just a little – more than you let anyone know?*

So far, this 'soldier' thing seems like something I might be pretty good at. But I'm afraid the details may seem a bit gruesome. We've marched from Italy through the western edge of Switzerland into France. Once we reached France, most of the platoon felt that we were "home free and clear" – safe from the enemy. Thurman Parker and me, we both knew better. (I'll tell you about him, and Rossi, in a minute). Even the Captain has acted like we're on our way to a Saturday night social without the pie auction. Rossi, Powell and I always spread out along the flank to keep an eye out for attacks from the rear. Two young Aggie Lieutenants on horseback would ride between us and the platoon. We all moved through the woods about 300 yards away from the road. The motor pool would go on ahead to help set camp for the evening. As I said, none of this was done quietly or with any sense of urgency. Day before yesterday, we'd finished breakfast, broke camp and just begun the day's march when shots rang out. Rossi happened to be driving the Sgt.'s Jeep so it was just me and Parker at the rear without Rossi for the day. At the first shot, I hit the dirt and looked to see if Thurman was okay. He was on the ground, too but waved so I'd know he was not hit. I crawled over to him then we looked toward the troops who had also hit the dirt. That was when we realized that one of the Aggies had been shot, falling from his horse and that the other one, Lt. Couples, was nowhere to be seen. Even his horse, Ginger, was gone. We slowly stood up and ran to Lt. Berry then…Look at me, giving you all the ugly details that will likely be censored out – from what I hear. Let me get to the point! We spotted a rough trail for the missing Lieutenant so we high tailed it back to platoon camp. Major called in a specialty team from Headquarters back in Italy to lead a search for Lt. Couples. The leader of the team was a WOMAN. A Master Sergeant Helen Taylor who was homely as a mud fence but she knew how to ride a horse and bark out orders. Rossi, Thurman and I got sent with the group because we knew where the 'evidence' was from the day before. After walking around the woods, the creek and the camp field, and finding hardly any real clues, the lady Sgt. decided there was some big espionage plan. I disagreed so we got turned crossways. I called the Major and he ordered us back to camp. Sgt. Taylor was real mad but she didn't say anything. (I'll probably get in trouble later – maybe court martialed). That's pretty much the same as getting fired from a normal job.

 Just so you have an idea of how we spend most days; I'm the company clerk. This means I'm responsible for ordering supplies – everything from spark plugs to powdered milk to cotton bandages – and I get to use the 10 pound radio phone quite a bit. Thurman Parker and Rossi (who refuses to admit to having a first name) are the two fellow privates that I'm around most. Both are east Texas natives and came through boot camp, same as me, though we didn't all meet up until Italy. Rossi is an aide to the officers – driving them around and stuff. A little bitty guy who flits around like a gnat, totes that dang telephone and tends to everyone else's business. Likeable little fellow. Parker is a tall, lanky drink of water. Slow talking, slow walking. He's forever shaking a dried acorn with the cap still on. It's a funny thing. A little odd. He reminds me of Slick except Thurman is sharp as a new pencil. Usually if you see one of us, you'll have all three of us. Not sure why, it just happened. I'd trust either of them with my life; same as they trust me. Sure hope I don't have to, though.

 Right now, Major has us preparing to roll out tonight, headed to our rendezvous with the Allies. Wish I could tell you where we are but I really don't know. Wish I could tell you where we're going but I don't actually know that, either. Wish I could tell you why we're here but nobody seems to know that.

 What I really want to say is that I miss you – you, Em. Sure I miss the kids and home. Much more than you'll ever believe but it's true what they say. 'You don't know what you've got until it's gone.' What I really hope is that *when I get back to Texas, you'll let me come home. What I really hope is that I can get to know my children again – and that they can get to know me. I know you believe a leopard doesn't change its' spots but I have changed – a lot. What I really hope is that you'll let me prove it.*

Gotta run now, Em. We're loading up to roll out tonight. Real battle is about to start. I wish I knew what we're fighting about. So ….until I get home……

Love you and Hugs to all from your husband,
Charlie Clarence Jones

Clarence folded the letter into a square and tucked it into his shirt pocket, wondering where Rossi and Thurman had gotten off to. About the time he rebuttoned his pocket, Thurman ambled up, "What're you up to there, ol' man? Writing a letter to that cute little wifey of yours?"

Clarence came up off the bench, suddenly angry.

"What are you asking about my wife for? She's none of your concern so I'd suggest you choose your words carefully."

"Easy there, Clarence. Nothing personal. Just a passing remark. We need to get to work back there with Cookie."

Clarence took some slow deep breaths, realizing his reaction was unreasonable.

Maybe the tension of the situation was grating Clarence's nerves more than he realized. Maybe he missed the farm, the family – even Slick, much more than he dreamed possible. Maybe he was scared but just not willing to let that surface because if he did, he might be paralyzed with it. It could be that he felt a sense of responsibility to those around him now; something that he'd tried to escape. Clarence apologized then he and Thurman fell in helping to set out K ration tins for evening mess. Rossi joined in shortly, finishing up tasks as Cookie assigned them. All the men ate quickly and quietly because they knew the night would be a long one, leading them into situations they'd just as soon avoid.

Then, a strange thing happened. Instead of leaving the mess tent for somebody else to clear, all the men took their empty tins and utensils out back. They threw away the tins and washed the forks, knives and spoons in the tubs. Then they sorted the cutlery into boxes and began breaking down the tables, all without direction from Cookie or the Major. Rossi took off at a trot to the motor pool to get the mess trucks so loading could begin. In the ten minutes he took, the tent was dismantled. As soon as Rossi pulled up, everyone fell in loading. Clarence and Thurman boxed dry goods from the 'pantry' while Cookie stood back with his mouth hanging open. Rossi pulled the packed truck forward so Morgan could bring up the next one. In less than 60 minutes, the entire camp was totally broken down. Clarence patrolled the area to make sure nothing was dropped, missed or abandoned that might be considered confidential.

Major stood staring at the men working in wordless focus and coordination. As Clarence walked up to report the area as cleared, Major said, "Looks like you soldiers have finally become brothers. And not a minute too soon."

Rossi pulled up in the Major's Jeep and as he hopped in, he called out, "Private Jones . . . Good work, man. You're an excellent soldier and, I suspect, a pretty decent human being. Take care of yourself in the next few weeks. I hear you've got a family waiting back in Texas. Rossi, what're you just sitting there for, boy? Shoot some gas to this bucket a bolts and let's roll."

Rossi sniffled, wiped his nose on his sleeve then roared ahead to lead the caravan.

It was Clarence's turn then to stand with his mouth hanging open. Thurman strolled up, clapping a hand on Clarence's shoulder, "My stars and garters. Thought Major was gonna kiss your ring. But, I believe his opinion to be accurate. Now, before it gets too gushy, let's jump on one of these trucks and see if we can figure out where the hell we're going. Here, I picked up a couple of envelopes from the officers tent when we were packing up. They may be useful if you intend to mail your letter."

"Thanks, Parker. You're all right. I don't care what anybody else says."

With that, they jumped on the back of the last truck to join the parade, scooting down into piles of canvas and small folding chairs. Turned out they'd hitchhiked onto the truck loaded with the officers tent paraphernalia where they would spend most of the next eight weeks. Major was making up for some lost time, it seemed, because all meals was served off the back of the mess truck, even when they did stop for the night. Only the small metal, divided plates were used and each soldier was responsible for their own. Cookie didn't have to do dishes on this march. No cots unloaded and no fires built. And they never pitched camp at night. Turns were taken driving so they could keep moving. Rossi stayed busier than a one legged man in a butt kicking content making sure that the vehicles were all running smoothly. This leg of the march, the platoon moved like a Swiss train.

Long days faded into weeks. Weeks counted by to become months. The 97th had moved so slowly before Major took over that they had almost two thirds of the trip yet to complete. They only stopped about every fifth night so the men could stretch out in the woods to sleep rather than all bunched up in the trucks. Even so, many of the young men stiffened with arthritis when cold weather set in as they moved toward their second winter in France.

It was hard not to compare winters in Europe with winter in Texas. The holiday season back home could just as easily be spent outdoors, pitching a baseball around the front yard with all the cousins as it could be passed in the house in front of an open log fireplace. But in France, you could just about count on nearly freezing your toes, fingers and nose most every night.

Thanksgiving and Christmas slipped by without much recognition – at least, none that any of the men felt like mentioning. With them on the move, no mail or packages were being delivered. Cookie managed to make some pretty good cornbread dressing which took them all back to Texas.

On January 10, 1918, the platoon arrived at the pre-determined rendezvous location. A solid week ahead of the due date. Major fully intended to dig trenches and have the site battle ready by the time the British Allies arrived. The 97th platoon and the incoming Allies would be the newest addition to more than 9,000 soldiers already stationed in Picardie.

The Americans were ordered to set up the mess tent and the officer's field tent. Then they were allowed to take the 11th to rest up. Clarence addressed another letter to Emily, sealed it and gave it to Rossi to be included in the official outgoing mail.

0500 mess on the morning of January 12 found every soldier on full alert with Major Eckhart, Captain Stutz – in a wheel chair - and Sgt. Odell there, huddled around the coffee pot. As soon as all trays were full and the men seated, Major stood up to announce the plans.

"I've decided that we are going to have those trenches ready before our new British friends arrive so we've got some serious digging to do. At 0600, Privates Jones, Thurman and Rossi report to my office to pick up the measurements and location map for the new trenches. As soon as those are marked, we'll get to work. Yes "WE." Sgt. Odell and I both know how to use a shovel, too. Captain will be supervising this effort. Now, let's show our appreciation for Cookie and eat up."

So they did. By 0630, everyone except Cookie and Captain Stutz were wielding shovels, hard at it. Even though this was his own idea, Clarence was not happy about it. He didn't mind the work but dang it, his shirt was filthy by 0730, soaked in sweat and he smelled like a mangy goat. The wet shirt just intensified the sting of the cold air.

But, Clarence knew they had more than two miles to dig and less than 180 able bodied men to do it so there was no other choice. The platoon put in a solid ten days and the trenches, or as some would say 'ditches' were finished the day before the British soldiers arrived on January 22, 1918.

The trenches were located about 2,500 yards west of the Sommes River bank… a distance deemed far enough to put the men out of range of most of the German weaponry. With the Allies alongside, everyone began cutting timber for lumber to reinforce the dirt walls and the ends of some the V-shaped trenches. The allies had brought thin, corrugated metal for this purpose but it was used instead to cover the end sections on some of the trenches to create sort of underground lean-to shelters. Some of these shelters were used as gathering sites for the officers.

On the third day after the arrival of the British brigade, just before Reveille, shots from the east rained down on the camp. The attack seemed to be targeted toward the mess tent, causing disruption but not doing any lethal damage. If it had been staged a half hour later, the impact would've been massive. As it turned out, Cookie was the only man in the tent. He got bruised a bit when a couple of tables and a tent pole fell on him but otherwise, he was fine and just as short tempered as ever.

At first nobody could believe Cookie was really okay, but they were convinced when he announced, "You all don't think a couple of bouncing bullets fired by them German sumbitches gonna disable this ol' cook, now do you? Let's eat!" But noon and evening mess was prepared and served by Rossi, Morgan and three other Privates as Cookie said he was feeling sore and could use a rest. Next morning's breakfast mess found Cookie back in the kitchen serving up the usual powdered eggs & dried mystery meat.

Then another 1000 Brits arrived. Thankfully, they brought another mess tent and three truck loads of dry goods. All of the men fell in digging more of those narrow trenches and extending the ones already in place. The Allied soldier count was now in excess of 11,000 – or 12,000 if you included the French.

On January 28th, another three days, and more shots rang out at dusk. A short but intense volley. Cookie said, "There's so many of us here now, they're bound to hit somebody ... and they did. Four killed – all British. Rossi was wounded. But it was just a nick, needing nothing more than a band aid on his neck.

Clarence declared, "Boy, you are one lucky little Eye-talian, that's all I got to say. If you weighed five more pounds, that shell would've done serious damage. As it is, you're barely going to have a scar."

Rossi bit back, "I'm not Eye-talian, dang it. I'm a Texan, sure as shootin' . . . same as you."

Clarence got to thinking about the two attacks since the British troops arrived. The pattern was the same as when Lt. Couples disappeared. He stewed on it for several days then went to the Major, sharing his opinion and ideas.

"It seems to me that maybe we *are* being stalked. It does chap my behind a bit to consider that Major Taylor *may* have been right. My bet is that there's just a handful of Germans camped somewhere in the woods over yonder by the river. They're assigned to try and draw us out in search of Lt. Couples and then they can grab a few more of us. But I think we can out maneuver them, though. And here's how." Clarence pulled out some paper and a pencil to sketch out his plan for the Major.

Major listened, agreed then assembled a team. With Clarence, Thurman, the Major himself, five sharp shooters and two medics, a team was formed. Rossi was miffed that he wasn't to be part of the group but Major assured him that staying in camp to help Cook and Captain Stutz if anything happened while the team was out on the search was just as important. Besides, if something went wrong with the mission, Rossi would not be 'guilty by association.' Major pointed out that none of the Allies were going to be involved, either since this would be a rogue action, not sanctioned and likely frowned upon by Headquarters.

Turned out, Major really was a pretty good ol' boy after all!

On foot, with packs personally loaded by Cookie, the team left that night about 2330, on foot, heading east roughly toward the river. Clarence told the men to proceed quietly but with urgency; that he would lead them in a serpentine pattern. And off they went through the moonless dark night. The soldiers were excited about being involved in any type of action so they hardly noticed that the inky black, cold night had passed by. Just before dawn, Clarence stopped the team close to a trickling brook but still under dense cover of woods. The group settled in to catnap, eat a bite and wait out the long day for another night to restart the search.

After dark and on the march again for only about two hours, they picked up the woody aroma of a campfire long before they spotted its' soft orange glow. Clarence stopped the team to scout ahead, alone. He spent most of the rest of the night crawling toward the woody smell of that campfire. He never once thought about his shirt.

When he finally spotted 12 German soldiers – no officers, he almost shouted out a loud "Yee Haw!" Shockingly, there sat Lt. Couples hunkered close to the campfire, head in his hands, looking miserable but unharmed. Clarence struggled to keep calm and not jump up. Instead, he cautiously slithered back to his team to report the findings to the Major.

Instantly, Major wanted to charge the group. But with Thurman's help, Clarence argued him out of that notion.

With the butt of his rifle, Clarence cleared sticks and leaves to create a smooth dirt surface. Then, he used the tip of the bayonet to draw out his idea for Major and all the other members of the team. After a rigorous debate, Major agreed that Clarence's plan should accomplish their mission without any additional injuries or worse, losing Couples life.

Eager to rescue Lt. Couples, it was difficult for the men to wait for the Germans to fall quiet on yet another, the third night in the field. At last, the team began the grueling crawl through the underbrush in the woods to reach the enemy camp. Though relaxed and quiet, the Germans were not sleeping; they were just sitting by the fire, oblivious to anything that might be going on outside of that halo of flickering warm light. The Sommes River was very nearby and at this point, it was no longer a shallow, trickling creek. It had turned itself into a narrow, 30 foot deep canyon filled with raging white water. The noise helped cover the accidental sounds of Clarence and team cracking and snapping their way through the woods on their bellies.

Following the plan, the team of ten Texans from the A&M 97th regiment spread out, encircling the camp while Clarence and Thurman crept around to position behind Lt. Couples. They quickly jerked him backward to the ground with hands over his mouth. He went limp as a dishrag, putting up no struggle. After all, this was the second time he'd been taken hostage in less than a month so he may have thought the path of least resistance was his best course of action; or, more likely, he just didn't have any fight left in him.

As soon as Couples hit the dirt, Major gave the 'fire' order. Not a single shot was returned and in less than 30 seconds, Lt. Couples was freed, four enemy soldiers were mortally wounded and eight were taken prisoner. The group began the march back through the woods, heading toward the road. With the prisoners carrying the bodies of their fallen comrades, progress was slow.

Much to the Major's surprise, a U.S. Army truck was idling about 30 yards to their right. Rossi had figured everyone would be worn out and Lt. Couples wouldn't be up to a ten mile march back to camp. Delighted when they heard the rumbling engine of that old Liberty Truck, the guys eagerly piled in, prisoners shoved in back first so they would be hemmed in without an option to jump. Then the casualties were loaded in next. They rolled back into camp around 0400 to a roaring ovation by Cookie, Sg. Odell and about 200 of the British allied troops.

Next morning, Cookie delayed Reveille to 0600 so 'the boys and Lt. Couples could rest up.'

The British soldiers were quite impressed with the rescue mission as they listened to Rossi tell tales as if he personally had been in the middle of the rescue.

The troops spent two quiet days; whiling away the hours reading or writing letters to send back home. A supply truck rolled into camp bringing a big green canvas bag of mail. Clarence was over the moon when he was handed a letter from Emily. He stared at her small, terse handwriting on the envelope for several minutes before carefully opening it. As brief in her writing as she was in her speech, the note simply read, "Come Home." After studying those two words for about fifteen minutes, he grinned to himself, carefully re-folded the note and buttoned it into his left shirt pocket. Rossi watched him read and re-read the letter and, though curious, he knew not to ask Clarence anything about it. But he was tickled to see that smile.

Somebody brought out an old baseball that had been tucked into a duffle for a couple of years and Cookie quickly produced a 'bat' so a rousing game of sandlot baseball broke out. No one was surprised that long, tall Thurman turned out to be a hotshot pitcher, throwing strike after strike. The British soldiers made a pretty good cheering section though few of them actually knew much about the details of the game. The prisoners watched, amazed, from the stockade tent. They didn't understand the game at all but it looked like fun.

After about two hours of rigorous play, Cookie declared a tie and called an early evening mess. With full bellies and tired muscles, the men slept soundly – until around 0400 the next morning, February 1st, when artillery fire from deep in the woods, opposite side of the river, shook everyone awake. It was a quick but deadly attack. A corner of the mess tent was shredded but the stockade tent took the brunt of the shelling. Before the dust could clear, Clarence, Rossi and Thurman careened into the Officers tent. Already there, was Major Eckhart, Lt. Couples, the British officers and even Captain Stutz, now up on crutches. Also gathered in the 12 foot square tent were two of the platoon medics, looking grim.

"Casualties?" questioned Thurman.

"Nowhere near as bad as it could have been. All the POWs were killed. We have four seriously wounded. Lost 2 mares and a Jeep. Cookie took flying shrapnel from some destroyed coffee pots. The worst problem, though, will be the potential for infection," replied the Medic.

Rossi asked, "You think it's retaliation for us bringing back the Lt. and taking those guys prisoner?"

"Of course," replied Major. "But, they killed their own men. We better get ready for a serious barrage soon. Let's make sure the trenches are supplied with ample water, ammo and hard tack – enough to last for at least a week. Clarence, get with Cookie to find out what we need. Rossi, you check with the motor pool boys. Thurman, get with the Allies non-coms to line up labor. We need to make sure the trenches covered space is readied. But first, we'll take the German bodies over to the river bank so they can be retrieved for their families. It's the Christian thing to do." When this task was finished, Major offered up a prayer and the safety of all soldiers – those on both sides of the Sommes.

Another quiet week passed while the Americans and the Allies worked at a quick, steady pace. Readied and tired of the suspense of waiting, on February 8th, 1918, the Allies initiated shelling. Grenade launchers and cannon fire took the Germans by surprise. They were used to being the aggressors so they were not ready.

But within 25 minutes, the Germans began to return fire without ceasing. With tanks clearing the way for the foot soldiers, they steadily moved toward the Allies until there was only a space of about 100 yards separating the two armies. With the Germans this close, the Allies were trapped in the bunkers and easily picked off if they tried to move from one trench to another.

The fighting continued virtually nonstop for the next three days when the Germans suddenly ceased fire. An uneasy quiet fell across the Sommes River valley.

Everybody held their breath, waiting. Finally, a head popped up over the edge of a trench. Then another and another. Until word came down from Major, relaying the call "Stand down, Men." Soldiers began climbing out into the strangely clear, still air. Officers walked about, surveying the damage and to count the casualties which numbered in the hundreds. The wounded, even more. Rossi was wounded again though still not enough to get him sent home. For this, he was thankful. Clarence took some powder burns to his hands, arms and chest from being so close to the cannon fire. But once he determined that his note from Emily was intact, his biggest personal concern was the ruination of his shirt. Thurman didn't have so much as a hair out of place. And that dadgum acorn still rattled!

Everyone knew that this cease fire was a ruse and wouldn't last more than a day, if that. Immediately, work began to reset for battle. Clarence resumed his Company Clerk duties. He didn't wait for an order from Major to restock medical supplies, ammunition of all types and groceries. He also ordered paper and envelopes, pens, stamps – and Bibles. He felt that it was past time for every soldier to have that little New Testament in their pockets.

This nervous calm lasted for five days with a few symbolic shots fired by both sides, just to let the other side know they weren't forgotten. As the supplies arrived, Clarence figured that the Germans were restocking as well though it was a little easier for the Allies since they were backed up to the road so trucks could get to them. The Germans had to wait for small boats and mule packs to bring the things they needed.

But that position also made them an attractive target for it was easy to attack them from the rear as they defended the forward assault. More critical still was the fact that, if the Allies lost this position, the Germans would gain access for an unrestrained march across to the West of France. With roads and river travel, they would be able to roll right across Europe, leaving nothing but scorched earth destruction in their wake.

"And for what?" wondered Clarence for the hundredth time.

Breaking into Clarence's thoughts one day, Thurman was unusually somber. He asked, "You have any plans for when this mess is finally over?"

Clarence quickly and earnestly replied, "I'm going back home to be a husband and father to my family."

"Where did you say you're from?"

"From Van Zandt County, Texas. Same as you. You know that. What's wrong with you?"

"I'm from Henderson County.

"So what? That's just the next county south from Van Zandt. We could still be neighbors. Say, what're your plans once we leave this lovely vacation spot? You going back to Texas?"

"Oh sure, I'll go back. Can't imagine calling any place other than Texas home. But farming? I'm not sure about that. Lots of other options will be opening up for us 'brave old soldiers' so we'll just have to see what happens."

Clarence commented, almost to himself, "It's odd. I left that life behind to find adventure – and to avoid responsibility. I told myself that I'd learn about the world, make some new friends and pick up new skills. And that part has held true. But in the process, I've seen some of those friends blown to bits, others maimed so that their future view will only be what they can see from a wheelchair. Nightmares that I may never shake. And responsibilities to you guys that have proven far heavier than anything I left back in Van Zandt county, Texas."

Thurman, sounding more like his normal self, replied, "And don't forget. You've had to wear dirty shirts far too often."

Clarence, breaking into a grin, "You dumb ass. I'm being serious here."

"I can't wait to get home to Emily and the kids. I can't wait to get a crop in the field. Probably tomatoes – maybe peas. Black-eyes, Crowder, Purple Hull. I can't wait to eat Emily's cooking – cornbread, coconut cake, pork chops and fried chicken."

"Stop! Now, I'm starving. Can I go home with you?"

"Sure – but you can't stay there at the house. It's bursting at the seams already. But Slick, my brother-in-law, Emily's brother, lives barely a mile down the road. He and his wife, June, have plenty of space. And no kids. He could always use an extra hand. Hell, I'll need some help, too."

Thurman paused to give this joking idea some serious consideration as he rattled that acorn. "Hmmmm. Got no actual family of my own – yet. I might just do that."

Suddenly, just before evening mess, incoming artillery fire put an end to contemplation of the future, this time catching the Allies off guard. Before the men could even begin diving into the nearest foxhole, casualties started mounting – again. The Major was hit but Lt. Couples managed to duck into a covered trench where he headed straight to the back. Capt. was still on crutches and slow moving but the British officers were scrambling to establish some sort of orderly return fire.

The attack was making quick work of the dugout foxholes. It seemed as though the trenches were the actual targets.

With this volley, Cookie was killed.

Clarence, Rossi and Thurman ran through open fire to dive in and pull Lt. out of the covered pit which turned out to be a pure death trap. Lt. Couples resisted them, hunkering at the far end, still traumatized after his prisoner of war incident. He wouldn't voluntarily give up what he thought was a safe spot so Clarence and the boys had to drag him, kicking, out into the open trench. Couples then rolled into a ball with bullets screaming overhead, artillery fire hitting so close that the ground shook, and causing the men's bodies to vibrate like a thousand tiny springs had been injected just under the skin. Dirt and smoke filled the air, burning their eyes and lungs. Adding to the blindness was rolling sweat. Sweat from manhandling the cannons back and forth to scatter fire; Sweat from wrestling the bandolier ammunition belts. No one could actually see what they were firing at. They could barely tell which direction they needed to aim toward.

But thicker than the smoke and sweat was fear, fear so dense you could smell it. A kind of fear that determines your future. It either freezes you in place and kills you, if not right at that moment then surely in years to come. Or you rise to it, usually without deliberation. You spring into action that saves your life and all the rest of your days ahead.

Just as the three men got Lt. Couples out into the open trench about 20 yards down, a grenade landed on top of the covered tin roof where they'd all just been. They were pelted by rocks, dirt and shrapnel but surprisingly, a portion of the makeshift roofing held up, shaking but intact.

Clarence lost his grip on Lt. Couples' belt, dropping to his knees and falling forward. Thurman and Rossi both let go of Couples to grab Clarence.

The back of Clarence's shirt was dotted with tiny holes; his neck covered in speckles of blood.

Couples scrambled to his feet and, for the first time in the weeks since his abduction, gathered his wits and assumed his duties. He shouted, "Get Jones inside."

Clarence shouted, "No, that place is a tomb. I'm fine right where I am," as he patted his shirt pocket. "Get down low. We're gonna need you. The boys and I will go to work about thirty yards down. See that Howitzer? That's where we'll be. You can scramble to us if you need to but stay low and keep your wits about you!"

Clarence turned to Rossi and Thurman, "Okay boys. Here we go. Grab anything along the way that fires bullets. The Howitzer is pointed toward the River – let's heat up that barrel like a Saturday night hooker."

"Yes, Sir!" from both Thurman and Rossi.

With shells whistling just above their heads, Rossi took on the roll of assistant gunner, moving the M40 left and right while Thurman moved it up and down. Rossi bent to grab a length of M106 ammo and just as he stood back up, he saw Thurman go down, taking a severe hit.

Rossi began to panic, crumpling to the ground with a low moan. Clarence was having none of Rossi's theatrics just now so he yelled, "Get a grip, kid. You can moan later – if you're lucky." He then ripped off his shirt to bandage Thurman's left arm. Judging from the damage, Clarence thought it was a useless effort but he knew Thurman would do the same for him.

At that same moment, Lt. Couples appeared through the smoke, grabbing Rossi, "Okay, Rossi, let's play soldier. Get on that barrel and hold 'er steady."

Another half hour and incoming fire finally began to slow then stop. An hour passed, all quiet. That skirmish had lasted four hours.

Clarence called out to Rossi, "Get that radio and call for a medic."

"Where are we?"

Lt. Couples shot back, "A half mile west of Hell."

Clarence: "About a quarter mile west of the Sommes River. Just south of Albert. Also let them know that the Major was hit but we don't know how badly and that, as far as we know, Lt. Couples is in charge of the entire platoon."

As Rossi grabbed the radio, rapidly cranking it for power, he mumbled, "Good Lord." Fumbling with the headphones, it took several minutes to raise a response from Headquarters in Italy.

"This is Rossi with the A&M 97th. Help us. We're pinned down a quarter mile west of the Sommes River, south of Albert. Dozens dead. Major Elkhart wounded. Lt. Couples in charge of this American platoon. No information on the British."

Cracking answer, "How long?"

Rossi, "Not sure. It's been at least two days." The response was nothing but static and try as he might, Rossi couldn't get anyone else to respond.

Lt. Couples, "We're on our own."

Clarence, "At this rate, we'll be out of ammo in another day, I'm not sure Thurman will last. He's lost an awful lot of blood. Rossi, no panicking on your part."

Just as Clarence was about to launch into a real butt-kicking, inspirational sermon, as much for Couples as for Rossi, shelling started again. But neither Rossi nor Clarence paid attention to anything but Thurman. Rossi pulled off his own shirt to add another layer to the bandaging. But as he did, he pulled a letter out of Clarence's shirt pocket that had already gotten a little blood stain on it. Sticking the letter into the radio case, he figured on giving it back to Clarence later.

Lt. Couples grabbed that Howitzer and, with a crazed grin, began an assault of his own.

Surprising every one, Major dropped down into the trench. Noting their expressions, "Sorry to disappoint you boys but I'm not dead yet." Then, Major leaned over and whispered to Rossi. Rossi managed a slight smile, turned to Clarence and said, "You and Couples got this by yourselves a minute, okay?" Then he jumped to the surface and took off at a quick low duck-like waddle with his knees even with his ears.

Major knelt down next to Clarence so he could speak to Thurman, "Hang in there, Parker. You're in good hands here."

Moving over to Lt. Couples, Major asked "How you?"

"Very well, Sir, maybe still a little nervous. Thanks for asking." as he slowed up firing for just a moment.

"Say, tell me what you think of Clarence there. For later, down the road."

"He's a good man. A good soldier, a good man. Kinda rogue for an officer but as a Non-Com, he'd be exceptional. I guess I might be just a little biased though."

Major's only reply was "Hmmmm" as he leapt out of the trench and headed off in the same direction that Rossi had taken.

After 36 hours of almost nonstop shelling, another uneasy calm followed. The British troops and Allies nervously celebrated. An American Captain from Headquarters in Italy arrived along with another mess cook, a full load of food and ammunition. Plus pens, paper, envelopes, stamps, Bibles . . . and shirts "that somebody keeps ordering." Medics made it to Thurman Parker in time to save his life, though not his arm. He was discharged and sent home to Athens, Henderson County, Texas.

On the fourth day of this cease fire, Major Elkhart with Captain Stutz by his side called "Attention, Men" during evening mess.

As the men quieted down, wondering what was going on, Captain Stutz, on just one crutch now, and Major Elkhart stood, calling Clarence up to the impromptu podium. He then pinned Corporal stripes onto one of those new shirts that Clarence had ordered.

The Major boomed out, "Corporal Charlie Clarence Jones is a good soldier. He has quietly gone about helping his fellow GIs and officers alike. Feeding, arming and in general keeping us moving. He was a good soldier beginning in boot camp right up through that 300 mile march from Italy into France. Since then Clarence has helped with injuries, a kidnapping and shell shock. He has encouraged others and through it all, wore clean shirts even when taking pellets in his own back and neck. For all that, we are also recognizing Corporal Jones with a Purple Heart. It is our hope and prayer that Clarence and all of you, safely return to your home soil. I'm proud of you, son."

Rossi was the first to his feet, leading cheers, whistles and applause. Everyone knew that Cookie would've been in the middle of the congratulations. The rest of the tentful joined the celebration and even the British troops started chanting "Speech, Speech."

Before Clarence raised his head then held his helmet in the air; His signature sign for 'Pipe down,' years of memories flooded through his mind. As far back as his own lonely childhood, fearing the nights when his papa roared into the house drunk as a skunk. The beatings his mama took for way too long then, the shock when his mama snapped and threw that black, cast iron skillet at papa. If only she'd missed – but she didn't. She hit him square in the middle of the back of the head. Papa was dead when he hit the floor. Of course, the sheriff took Mama to jail where she stayed for 14 years, until she died at the age of 42. Clarence was six months shy of his 12th birthday so he was sent to live with his mother's sister, an old maid, school teacher in Georgia. He met her for the first time when she picked him up at the train station. It was clear from the git-go that having Clarence in her house was not of her choosing.

As soon as he was old enough, he left Georgia, returned to Texas and boarded with a large, loud, happy family in Van Alstyne. There, he met Emily and married her. No one had ever, ever told Clarence that they were proud of him.

"Thank you Major Elkhart, Captain Stutz, Sgt. Odell, Lt. Couples, Rossi. Thanks also to Thurman Parker who was sent home to recuperate and to Cookie, who went to his Heavenly home. I'm sure he's fixing some wonderfully creative meals for all the old soldiers who were already there. And thanks to all y'all – your support and dedication has truly changed me. More than any of you will ever know." After a pause and clearing of his throat, Clarence continued. "I guess it's about time for me to tell y'all the truth. I enlisted in this Army because I was scared and running from responsibility. At 34 years old, I was running from being an adult – Y'all will think I'm the biggest coward in the world. For sure, I'm no hero. I left behind a wife and three kiddos – a 9 year old girl, Vada, on the way to becoming a fine young lady, a 7 year old – my boy, Bill – the smartest kid ever. And can he work! – Why you never saw the like. And a 2 year old blond charmer, Julia May, who'll never lift a hand at anything she don't want to. Plus, my wife had two older girls after burying their daddy and we'd also lost one baby boy to spinal meningitis. So, what did I do to help her with all this?

I ran. Ran out on her, leaving her with five children, a farm to tend, no money. But y'all have taught me to be a grown man. Look at you guys. Captain and Major, both injured but still at it every day. Cookie . . . showing up to serve his country long after he could have retired. Serving even to his last day on this earth. Lt. Couples going through serious trauma then covering us with fire until the situation calmed down. Each of you with your own story and battle, sacrificing for the rest of us. So… . At the end of this war that we don't understand, I'm going home with my hat in my hand. I'll beg forgiveness, kiss my wife if she'll let me, hug my children and never leave them again."

With that, Clarence brushed his cheek with the back of his hand, patted his shirt pocket and sat down.

Thunderous applause filled the tent.

Major reached for Clarence's hand, shaking it vigorously, patting the newly pinned stripes and even swallowed a tear or two himself.

Clarence grinned, shaking hands with Sgt. Odell who had been right beside him since the recruiting office in Athens. Lt. Couples grabbed the new Corporal in a huge bear hug, whispering "You saved me, man. Twice. I'll owe you forever." Rossi stood back, shyly waiting for Clarence to notice him. When he did, he put his arm around Rossi and said, "I'm proud of you, kid." Rossi teared up but ducked his head so no one would see. But Clarence did see. He told Rossi, "Here's another thing I've figured out. A few tears are okay, man. It lets people know you have feelings. It's nothing you need to hide. Nobody thinks any less of you over a couple of tears."

The British officers produced a vast amount of horrible wine that most of the men believed came out of Cookie's stash. Home brew that Cookie procured along the way when he was out hunting 'vegetables.'

Bad wine led to bad singing which lasted into the wee hours.

When the war is over
We're going to live in Dover,
When the war is over we're going to have a spree;
We're going to have a fight In the middle of the night
With the whizz-bangs a-flying in the air.

When the party finally wound down and the men began to hit their bunks, bugler played a heart-rending Taps. Everyone knew it was for Cookie and all the friends they'd lost in the last six months.

First Assistant in the kitchen had bugler play Reveille late, at 0600, just as he knew Cookie would've done it. The tent slowly filled; even all the Allied soldiers looking like 40 miles of bad road. Fortunately, the day progressed quietly. Lots of letter writing, stocking of the trenches and supply tents, stacking of ammo by the big guns, chitchat stayed at a minimum with the men trying to keep their nerves under control.

Clarence washed up that new shirt – the one with the Corporal stripes, smoothing and laying it on a tin roof to dry.

Then, the morning of February 25th, 1918, dawned with shells raining down like molten rocks and grenades landing every few feet. The German army had crept so close during the night that there was even some hand to hand bayonet fighting underway. Ready, the Allies slid into place, matching the Germans round for round. Two hours of fighting without a breather on either side. There were so many lives grenades on the ground, the Allies feared stepping out of their trenches into No Man's Land. Dogs were sent out as scouts to find bombs and to carry shells from trench to trench.

Horses were used to carry water, hard tack and larger shells to the trenches.

The firing continued for three days straight, both sides were fiercely determined to outlast the other. Finally, it stopped. Mostly because everyone was too exhausted to fire another round. At first, it wasn't obvious the number of casualties. When the dust settled, it was determined that the Allies had lost 5,000 men. The Americans made up 2,000 of that number.

Rossi was the first American to stand up and look out. He'd never seen such devastation in his life – not even after a tornado went through Paris, Texas when he was ten years old. Looking east toward the Sommes River, there were no trees left. There was nothing but death – men, horses, dogs. Pools of blood glimmered like mirages in the dust filtered sunlight. Rossi now knew what people meant when they said something was 'deathly silent.'

Leave the Lamp On...

Feeling sick to his stomach, he turned his attention back into the trench. A German soldier lay dead, no more than six feet from where he stood. The German lay face down but was bunched up as though he was lying across a duffel bag. Stepping closer, Rossi could tell that the German was lying across another body. Rossi kicked the German away, finding Clarence staring up at him, lifeless.

Remaining uncharacteristically calm, Rossi determined that Clarence had been stabbed in the back but must have turned in time to get a point blank shot off at the German. Leaning down to straighten his collar, he put that letter to Emily back in Clarence's left shirt pocket. Then, he realized that wouldn't do so he took the letter back, tucking it into his own shirt. When he pulled it out a second time, another letter came out with it. Rossi looked at it and saw the tiny, neat handwriting that said "Come home." He tucked it away with the answer that Clarence didn't get to mail. Working his way from one end of the 100 yard trench to the other, Rossi discovered that he was the sole survivor there. The total lack of sound unnerved him as much as anything else.

He slide down the trench wall to a sitting position, confused, scared, suddenly so alone. What would he do without Clarence to guide him? His sense of obligation to Clarence was overwhelming. What would Emily and all those children do if Clarence didn't come back home?

Rossi was only 18 years old. He'd lied to get into the Army. He was a farm boy with a talent for fixing anything with a motor; Cars, trucks, tanks or as it turned out, airplanes – anything that had wheels so he had skills the military needed. This prompted the recruiting officer to look the other way as far as his age was concerned. Rossi had idolized his Italian immigrant father but "Pops" died when Rossi was only four so his memories were dimming with time. Finally, Rossi thought of Clarence's words about "No time to panic" and "I'm proud of you" so he stood up to survey the surroundings for other survivors. He stumbled into Major Eckhart who was also badly shaken.

"We've lost so many, many men."

"And Clarence."

Both men dropped to the ground, unwilling to consider what should be done next. Finally, Rossi said, "Request permission to take Clarence home, Sir."

Major responded, not unkindly, "No. He will be buried here, in country, in a special place. A place that will be remembered for generations; long after you and I are gone from this earth."

After while Rossi asked, "What do we do now, Sir?"

"Fall forward. Always, fall forward, Rossi." Then Major went on to continue his review, leaving Rossi to ponder what 'Fall Forward' meant.

A British cook picked up mess duties. Some of the soldiers wandered around, retrieving mementos and trinkets where they could. Items to be saved or sent home to families. The soldiers worked as a team and by early afternoon, they came across six Germans, wounded and scared but alive. A medic was called to patch them up to take them as prisoners.

Major and the Allied officers spent time discussing the next offensive steps. They planned to attack on the 15th – the Ides of March seemed appropriate - but the Germans launched a new assault on the 14th. An assault that was badly planned and poorly supplied. Within a day, the Germans simply quit shooting and began to retreat. Once this happened, they didn't stop backing up and on April 1st, 1918, the Germans surrendered. In the almost ten months of battle along the Sommes River, over one million casualties had been suffered.

Corporal Charlie Clarence Jones was buried in the Sommes American Cemetery in Picardie, France along with 1,844 of his fellow soldiers.

Thurman Parker, back home in Texas, did recuperate from the loss of his arm. He was forever proud of his military service but he did not go back to the farm. He took advantage of the surging popularity of the automobile and took a job selling Chevrolets in Athens. Thurman sold cars, and rattled acorns in his pocket for the next 70 years, living to the ripe old age of 96. He married, had one daughter and built a lovely home that still stands in Athens today.

Most survivors limped home to welcome parades, cheers and open arms. Many of them were teenagers when they left but old men when they returned.

Rossi went back to Paris, Texas to his Mama's house. He ate like a horse but slept fitfully, if at all, for about two months. He had no interest in going to town or visiting with old friends. He no longer had anything in common with them. This worried his mother, Estaline, to no end. She was a robust, friendly woman who knew everyone in the small farming community of Paris in northeast Texas.

One sunny morning in July, he got up when he smelled bacon cooking and coffee perking. When his mother sat down to watch her boy eat, Rossi glanced up and said, "I'm leaving for awhile today, Ma. Got something that I need to tend to."

With a sigh, his mother simply said, "I know, Son. Will you be back?"

"I'm not sure. If I stay there, I'll let you know where I am. If I don't, you'll know it soon enough when I show back up. Either way, there won't be nobody shooting at me, that's for dang sure."

Emily sat at the kitchen table watching Myrt, Virgie and Vada wash the supper dishes and clean up the kitchen. As she watched them, she couldn't believe how they'd grown into young women, particularly Myrt and Virgie. And Bill, well, what was she going to do with him? Now almost ten years old, he worked as hard as any three grown men. She needed that work but she felt guilty, a little, that he was having no childhood at all. Plus, she already knew that she'd need to keep him out of school – again - come next spring to begin clearing the extra land she'd bought. Bill had done such a good job bringing in last year's tomato crop then selling them at the First Monday market in Canton, she was able to pick up another five acres of good sandy soil; Perfect for more tomatoes. Even Julia May was growing up. At age six, she was already proving to be mostly useless. She refused to do chores, wouldn't turn her hand to do anything, no matter how many spankings she got. Emily thought to herself that she hoped Julia married well because she sure wasn't going to know how to work at anything to take care of her own self.

Lost in thought, a shadow crossing the porch brought her back to the present. She started to the door just as a soft knock came. She flipped on the living room lamp and gasped at the young man standing there. In full Army uniform displaying Private stripes and his Overseas War chevron patch on his left sleeve, he still looked to be barely more than a boy.

Silently staring at Rossi for a full minute before regaining her composure; "You knew him?" Emily asked.

"Yes, Ma'am. May I come in?"

"Let's sit on the porch," as Emily stepped through the door. She turned back toward the kitchen. "When you girls are done, turn out the lights and head to your room. Don't malinger. I'll be along directly." Before moving to her porch rocker, she picked up some mending from the sewing basket next to her chair. Sufficient light for sewing was already gone but Emily needed something to still her hands.

"You came to talk?" she asked.

Rossi cleared his throat and mentally questioned the purpose of his visit. "I think so, yes, Ma'am. I came to make sure you knew that Clarence died a hero, a good man and a good soldier. He had every intention of coming home to you and the family. Of making sure they grew up straight and strong. And that they knew they were cared for. And you, too, ma'am, if you don't mind me saying."

Emily seemed to soften just a bit. Rossi thought he could sort of see it. She said, "I don't mind. How do you know these things about Clarence? Things I never knew."

"He told me – he told us all. The night he got his promotion from Private to Corporal. He told the entire platoon that he only joined the Army to get away from the farm. That he was afraid of the responsibilities. That he resented the expectations that everybody here had of him."

Emily couldn't resist a little, "Humph. I knew all that."

Undaunted, Rossi continued as though he was back in that mess tent, listening to Clarence talk. "He said that we'd all taught him to be an adult, a grown man. One who knew how to depend on others so others could depend on him. He talked about how he intended to come back here, run this farm the way he knew you would want it done, support his children and love all of you. And he meant every word."

Emily knew of the promotion. She learned of it when she got the Western Union telegram telling her that he'd been killed. "What'd he get promoted for?"

Rossi was glad to share the details of Clarence's abilities and efforts that began as far back as boot camp. He regaled her with the rescue of Lt. Couples, both times. Rossi left out nothing and, of course, like always happens; the heroics of a departed loved one are magnified many times over while their short-comings fade in the wash.

He hesitated, though, when the story arrived near the end. He knew Emily was up to hearing the bits and pieces but he was afraid he would crumble into a blubbering heap himself. Rossi had spoken to no one about finding Clarence dead. No one other than Major Elkhart knew the awful details they had memorized while they were still sitting in that narrow trench next to him and the equally dead German soldier.

Emily saw the young man's hesitation and realized that it was his own courage that needed a boost. "Buck up there, boy. Let's hear the rest of this story."

Rossi felt as though Clarence himself had just given him a poke in the arm. He chuckled a little, drew a big deep breath and said, "Yes, ma'am." Then he told her of Charlie Clarence's last battle. He left out none of the particulars and when he got to the part about finding the letters in Clarence's pocket, he pulled them out and handed the worn papers to Emily. Gentle like as though he were handing her a new butterfly. She took them in the same manner. "I'll read it later," Emily said, coughing just a little, tucking it into the bodice of her dress.

Uncharacteristically, she asked Rossi about his own life and what his future held. He told her everything, even his first name. Emily blurted out, "How old are you, boy?"

Rossi instantly replied, "19 years old, ma'am. But it feels like a lot longer." He told her about when his daddy died and how his own mama took the reins, raising him and running the farm alone. Emily said that it sounded as though she and his mama had walked a similar path. They talked 'til well after 11 o'clock when Slick startled them both, appearing on the porch steps without either Emily or Rossi hearing him approach.

Slick said, "I walked out into the road just to get a b-breath of air and c-check out the stars. It's such a clear night that I noticed the lamp still on and decided I better come see about my b-baby s-s-sister." For once, Emily didn't chastise him for meddling.

Instead, introductions were made and the conversation continued on awhile longer. Slick finally asked, "Y-young man, do you want to come up to my h-house for what's left of the night? My wife, June, is a m-mighty fine cook and you'd be more'n welcome. I'm about to d-d-doze off sitting here on these steps."

Rossi whispered to himself, "Cook" then glanced over at Emily for her reaction. She looked at ease with the notion and the big curly haired man seemed sincere, so, with only the briefest hesitation, Rossi accepted the offer. Besides, he felt as though he already knew Slick.

Slick stood up, "Well come on then. L-let's go to the house. I'll bet my June bug put some c-cake out on the table for a midnight snack." Rossi was now sure that he should go for the night.

As the two took off down the road, Emily sighed and went back into the house. 16 year old Myrtis was at the kitchen sink swishing a glass of water. She asked her mother, "Who was that cute soldier boy?" Emily curtly replied, "The soldier that was with Clarence in France when he was killed. Go back to bed."

Emily knew that Rossi was far more mature than his years but he would still be susceptible to the giggles of her three nearly grown daughters. She also knew that Slick and June would likely take to him like a duck to water and do all they could to convince him to stay. She was right on all counts.

Slick – and June, too – seemed to see Rossi as the son they didn't have but June sensed that they couldn't smother him with too much 'tending' after he had suffered through so much. Plus, he did still have his own mother. But Rossi loved the attention, from Slick especially so after about ten days and a little coaxing, he went back to Paris to let his mama know where he was going to be living.

Emily continued to have mixed emotions about Rossi being so close by but Myrtis and Virgie were both tickled to pieces. Myrt let 14 year old Virgie know real quick that she better stay away from Rossi; that "he's mine." And, sure enough, two years later, when Myrt was 18 and Rossi was 21, they married.

Spending almost as much time working Emily's farm as he did at Slick's, Rossi had already realized that if the marriage was to be a success, he would have to put some distance between them and Emily.

About three months after the wedding, June had everyone over for supper one evening. It was then that Rossi and Myrt announced they were moving to Compton, California, just outside Los Angeles. Emily instantly went into a fit, staging a fainting spell. Myrt continued eating the smothered pork chops and creamed potatoes while Slick "revived" his baby sister. Rossi also stayed focused on his plate.

In short order, Emily realized that Rossi wasn't falling for her theatrics so she launched into a tirade. "What do you mean, you're moving to California? Why would you try to kill me after all I've done for you?"

Rossi remained calm in his response. "I appreciate all that you have done, raising Myrt into the fine young woman and wife that I fell in love with. And, I sincerely appreciate Slick and June for taking me in, feeding me, giving me time to figure out who I am after that hellish war. But it's time for Myrt and me to be our own selves. To begin our own life and build our own future. I see that future in California. It's the fastest growing state in the US of A. People are flocking out West, especially to Los Angeles, from all over the world. And since aviation is the wave of the future, there will be a big demand for my mechanical skill. So. . .We're going." Emily sulled up but remained silent. She sat silent long after the table had been cleared and the family settled on the front porch to let supper . . . and the news, digest. She saw it as defeat; one of her own changing sides. Emily saw her all children's marriages as abandonment and was openly hostile toward the sons and daughter-in-law. This did not, however, keep her from later moving into the house with Vada and her husband, Fred Parks.

Rossi and Myrt did move to California where they settled and raised two children, a boy and a girl, of their own. Strangely, as adults, both those children moved back to Texas to live and raise their own families. Rossi was correct in his assessment of job opportunities. He was immediately hired by Hughes Aircraft where he worked for the next 47 years. Myrt came back to Texas to visit her sisters and Bill, and her mother, a few times but never stayed long, not even after Rossi died or when Emily passed away in 1953.

Virgil George – Dump - married Clyde Keller, settled in Fort Worth, Texas and raised 9 children. Virgie and Clyde made a rare couple indeed having two children who were both "Juniors." They had Clyde, Jr. and V.G. whose given name was actually Virgil George, Jr. – named for his mother!

Clyde was a hard working man, spending his days at the new Boeing plant in Fort Worth. He made just enough money to keep food on the table for their large family and to buy beer on the weekends for himself and his wheelchair bound brother, Jake, who lived next door. Truth be told, Clyde made more than 'enough' money for beer because he often came home so drunk he couldn't hit the ground with his hat.

Unfortunately, Clyde was an angry, mean drinker who took out his frustrations on his wife. For years, Virgie sported new bruises every Saturday or Sunday morning. Like so many women of the era, she simply accepted Clyde's behavior as normal and always promised to "do better" at whatever wrong he accused her of that week. She excused him in large part because he was good to children. He never raised a hand to any of them and even insisted that when meal time rolled around, all the children in his house be fed before any adult sat down to the table. But as the children grew into their teen years, times were changing, especially for women. Virgie's four daughters, Dorothy, twins Vada May and Ada Fay and Barbara Ann, set in on their mama about how badly she had been treated for more than 20 years. They read her magazine articles and made her watch news programs on the television set.

After awhile, the steady barrage by her girls began to have an effect on Virgie. She thought about what Emily would've done if her first husband, Homer Pilgrim, or Clarence Jones had ever raised a hand to hit her. Virgie knew that as far as Emily was concerned, any man that hit her would never see daylight to do it again. With this on her heart, she decided that she had taken her last beating from Clyde Keller so when he stumbled in the back door the next Saturday night, she was ready.

She took the usual slaps and curses but this time, she didn't try to get away. Instead, she danced her way backward from Clyde until she had him in the dimly lit bedroom where she let him continue to punch and hit her until he'd exhausted all his anger and energy. He collapsed on his back across the bed and within 15 minutes, the unconscious snoring began. Virgie knew that he wouldn't wake again until nearly noon Sunday morning so she launched her planned revenge. A lifelong quilter, Virgie had picked a needle and thread as her weapons of choice. She pulled the bottom sheet loose from the box springs, making sure Clyde's feet were on the bed then she began to run a basting stitch all the way around the four sides of the bed. It took her almost two hours but when she stood up, she had Clyde secured into the sheets like a stuffed sausage.

Stretching her back, and with a little half grin to herself, Virgie tucked the needle into the lapel of her shirt waist dress then reached into the closet, pulling out a baseball bat. Swinging that bat over her head, Virgie hesitated a few seconds while she stared at the lump in the bed. Those few seconds were enough to stop her from what surely would've been a life changing event for both of them. Virgie returned the bat to the closet then headed into the kitchen where she picked up her O'Cedar dust mop; the one with the long green galvanized handle and the heavy, string head.

Virgie took that dust mop back to the bedroom and proceeded to beat the living tar out of Clyde with it, using the stringed head. She worked that sewn up lump over from one end to the other, back and forth, several times to make sure she didn't miss a spot. When she found his head and face, she flipped that mop around to use the metal handle end "just for the fun of it." During the beating, Clyde never moved a muscle. When Virgie wore herself out, she flopped down in the chintz covered chair in front of the dresser, dropping the dust mop at her side. There she sat until daylight began peeping in through the east window and she could hear her teenagers stirring.

Virgie cooked the usual big weekend breakfast, putting bacon, eggs, grits, biscuits and gravy on platters for everyone to serve themselves. Then, just as Billy Jack finished saying grace, Clyde stumbled into the kitchen and said "Sure smells good in here. Is there enough for me, too? Or maybe just coffee for now?"

15 year old Barbara Ann, the youngest of the Keller kids, jumped up and cried, "Daddy, what on earth happened to you? Your nose is bleeding. Both your eyes are black and all swollen. Have you lost a tooth?!" Clyde looked startled and confused but managed to reply that "I guess I must've tripped on the sidewalk coming home from Jake's last night."

Virgie never looked up or said a word. She just continued ladling gravy onto a buttered biscuit. Clyde said nothing else but with a grunt, he slowly eased down into the first chair on the right side of the table, where Virgie usually sat but now, she was in his normal place at the head of the table. He didn't yet know what had happened but he did know, somehow, that his world was off kilter. Something had shifted in his household. He wasn't sure why but he felt powerless to return things to the previous balance.

Time proved Clyde right. He never touched another drop of alcohol, living to the ripe old age of 88. Also, going forward, Virgie still made the best banana pudding you ever tasted and took loving care of her family, including Clyde. But whenever a meal was served, Virgie sat at the head of the table.

Vada married Fred Parks, moved to Dallas and the suburban area. They had three children but like Emily before her, Vada suffered the loss of an infant, a baby girl named Martha Faye. But also like her mother, Vada just tightened her belt a notch and got on with life. She raised a son, Charles, and a daughter, JoAnn, both of whom adored her. Fred was an 'entrepreneur' long before there was such a thing so he was out of the house a lot. Fred was never afraid to try new projects and Vada always supported his efforts. Soon after World War II, Fred developed a refrigerated semi trailer and opened a body shop to build them. The business took off but, unfortunately, Fred did not file for a patent on the concept so it didn't take long before competitors were turning out a cheaper product. In less than five years, Fred decided to close the body shop.

Fred thought that a café would be a nice addition in the small community of DeSoto where they had settled. Serving breakfast and lunch, Fred's restaurant success was driven by the pies baked by his sister-in-law, Maggie.

Maggie baked 8 beautiful meringue topped pies every morning for the breakfast run. In such a small town, word of those pies spread faster than back row Baptist gossip. On more than one occasion, folks lined up on Maggie's back porch to wait for those pies to come out of the oven. People were so anxious for that gooey goodness that they helped carry the pies down the street, past the young preacher's parsonage and in the back door of the café.

Then, around 10 o'clock one morning after being open just over a year, the breakfast cook appeared at Maggie's kitchen door. It was summer so only the screen door was closed. Arndell hollered, "Miss Maggie. Miss Maggie! Come quick. Fred is real sick and asked me to come get you."

Maggie never paused. She yanked off her apron, sending it sailing to her own mother, Alma, who was spending a few weeks visiting with the family. "Mama, tend to Sue Helen. I'll be back as soon as I can." The screen door slammed shut and Maggie struck a trot down the street, covering the 300 feet or so by hitting just the high spots. Arndell was a tall, muscular man who had done heavy labor all his life and was in superb physical condition but he couldn't begin to keep up with 4 foot, 10 inch Maggie when she got high behind.

Clattering into the café's back door, Maggie shot through the kitchen into the small office on the far side. The 10 by 10 foot dimly lit room with a desk and a side chair also held a sofa. That's where Fred was laying when Maggie burst in. She immediately knew that "Fred is real sick" was a major understatement. His skin was the gray of a mourning dove; his face was covered with sweat and his breathing was so shallow that she wasn't sure he was actually taking a breath. "Arndell, go get the Doctor. Go right now." As Arndell took off, Maggie spied Junior Jones, the dishwasher, lurking just outside the door, trying his hardest to be invisible. She said, "Junior, run wet a clean towel in cold water, wring it out and bring it to me. Hurry now!"

Maggie scooched onto the sofa to sit down next to Fred, taking his hand. Junior appeared with the cold cloth so Maggie wiped Fred's face and neck then draped it across his forehead. "Junior, open that window so we can get some air flowing and turn on that box fan. Face it here directly toward the sofa."

Fred turned his gaze to Maggie and gasped, "Vada" as his hand fell from hers. At that moment, the town doctor, Grady Summers, stepped into the café office. He looked at Maggie's stunned expression then moved to stand beside the sofa. Dr. hated that he was going to be first one to speak those hateful words out loud so instead, he asked, "Where's Vada? And the boy?"

Maggie said, "Vada left for California early this morning?" Then, "Arndell, go get Charles. He's at home. Yes, I know they have a telephone but this is not the time for that. Just tell him that he's needed here."

The doctor gently laid Fred's hand across his waist then turned to sit down at the desk, pulling official paperwork out of his black leather bag. In those days, it was not necessary to call a county medical examiner to pronounce a person deceased. The first physician at the scene would complete the forms to file with the state and see that proper next steps were taken. Dr. Summers began the task while waiting for young Charles to arrive.

Maggie went to the front of the café to update the one waitress, Dottie. Letting her know that they should go on home and she'd send news as soon as she knew anything to tell. Locking the front door, she flipped the 'CLOSED' sign over. By this time, Arndell was back with 20 year old Charles.

Old Dr. Summers was great with children who had head colds but this part of the job had never been his strong point. He shuffled his feet, cleared his throat a couple times and turned to glance over at Fred. Charles, who had grown into an impatient young man, finally snaps out "So is Dad dead? What happened?"

Charles' short tone actually seemed to help Dr. Summers who replied, "Sorry son but yes, Fred passed from a massive heart attack. It was so quick, he didn't suffer. There wasn't anything that could've been done. Your Aunt Maggie was here with him." When it looked like Charles was about to faint, Maggie took him by the arm and led him into the oak desk chair.

Dottie hadn't left. She had lingered nearby, listening for details so she sat a glass of fountain Coke down in front of Charles, sweet tea next to the doctor and cup of black coffee close to Maggie, asking "Anybody want pie?" A chorus of "No!" rang back.

As Dr. Summers finished the paperwork, Maggie asked Charles, "How long will it take Vada to get to Myrt's? I know it won't be today." Charles almost smiled then said "No, but she'll try. She planned to spend tonight in Tucson. That's over half way then she'll only have about 500 miles tomorrow." Doc asked Charles if he knew what his mother would want to do as far as funeral homes were concerned. "That's really the only decision that needs to be made right now." Charles wordlessly shook his head.

Maggie said, "Doc, have him taken to Byrums over in Lancaster. It's the closest for the Parks family."

"Consider it done, Maggie. I don't mean to be unkind, but y'all need to clear on out of here so the funeral home people can work."

"Charles, you're going to have to call Myrt and tell your Mother what's happened. She can fly home then go back later and get her new car."

"Oh, Aunt Maggie Jo, I can't do that. I can't possibly call Mother and say Dad has dropped dead. You have to come on back home with me, now. Won't you please call her for me? You can come to the house and use our telephone. Please. Besides, JoAnn is going to be a mess when she gets home from school this afternoon. She's going to need you, too. Please."

Of course, Maggie went to the house to be with Charles and his teenaged sister, JoAnn. She held JoAnn while she sobbed over the sudden loss of her daddy then ranted with anger that her mother wasn't there when daddy truly needed her. Maggie called Bill, told him to bring Alma and Sue Helen so she would have to fix only one supper. Then she stayed with them for the night "just in case." The next day was long and horrible with nothing to do but wait. At last, it was late enough to call California.

Maggie dialed then waited for the staticky ring then Myrt's big "Hello." When Myrt heard Maggie's voice, heard her ask if Vada was there yet, she knew something terrible had happened. She hollered from the hallway into the kitchen, "Vada, get in here. You've got a call." Vada looked over at Rossi who sat at the table, tossing him the ladle from the pot of sauce she'd been stirring then went to take the telephone from Myrt. Rossi followed Vada with a chair where she sat down without looking. She held the phone, never saying a word. Myrt and Rossi knew that Maggie was talking – they could hear her but couldn't make out what she was saying - but after about three wordless minutes, Vada handed the receiver to Myrt and walked back into the kitchen.

Myrt spoke to Maggie, "What happened?" Maggie relayed the news again. "Thanks for letting us all know, Maggie. I guess we'll see you soon."

Vada spoke up, "I'll be leaving as soon as I take a bath and change clothes. It'll take a solid 24 hours to get back to Dallas. Myrt, go with me. You'll have to keep me awake. Rossi, you get a flight as soon as you can then I'll fly you both back home when all is said and done." Myrt and Rossi knew there was no point in arguing or offering advice. Vada's mind and resolve was unshakeable.

Around 2am, California time, the sisters climbed into Vada's new 1955 Chevrolet and headed for Texas. With stops only for gas, 23 hours later they pulled into the driveway in DeSoto.

Bill took care of his mother, Emily, until the age of 18 when in 1928, he married Maggie Jo Cranford. Bill's marriage was the hardest for Emily to bear since he was her only son. Emily had never been shy about expressing her displeasure over the marriages of her children but the fit she threw at Bill's wedding was legendary. It involved her flinging herself dramatically across the hood of the car in front of the courthouse in Athens, Texas all the while screaming that her son was being "kidnapped by that woman." Maggie was 14 years old. Even though Maggie was really still just a girl, she was strong willed and refused to let Emily come to live with them. She was allowed to visit but not stay. So, Emily moved in with Vada and Fred. Even so, Maggie and Vada remained best friends until Maggie died, 71 years later.

Bill did have a streak of Charlie Clarence in him, though he never would have admitted it if he'd been told as much. Bill moved his family often, sometimes suddenly; Always in pursuit of a better job, a better way to provide for his family. Maggie told the story about one time, in 1942; Bill was late getting home from work. When he came in, he had three of his co-workers with him. He had heard a rumor of steady work in Corsicana, about 20 miles west of their current home in Brownsboro. Maggie was shocked when, as soon as the supper dishes were done, the men began bringing in boxes so she could start packing. They had the entire house disassembled and loaded onto a borrowed truck by 9pm. Bill reported to the new job at Bethlehem Steel at 8am the next morning. There, during World War II, Bill learned to be a master welder. This skill served him well for the rest of his life.

Married 41 years when he died, Bill and Maggie raised four children. Bill encouraged all his children to get the best education they possibly could.

True to Emily's fears, Julia May "Sis" was lazy all her life but did not marry, as Emily hoped, someone who would lavish her with riches. She married Ebb Adair who always believed that "work" was a four letter word not fit for public consumption. Sis was so lazy, she wouldn't say "Sooey" if the hogs were after her. Raising five children, she and Ebb remained in East Texas as dirt farmers, making a paltry living off the land. Just as it always seems to be true in every family, Only one of their children left home to follow a hint of ambition. Eldest son, Wayne, left the day he finished high school, joining the Air Force where he built a successful 20 year career.

After the loss of Clarence, Emily never remarried. She farmed in Van Zandt County, Texas until the mid-1940's then moved to Dallas County to work land that her brother, Slick, had rented. As it turned out, neither of them knew how to make that gummy black land produce anything except Johnson grass so back to East Texas she went. Slick and June stayed in the Dallas area but Slick gave up farming altogether. He went to work for Chance Vought, an upstart in the aviation field. June got a job with AT&T as a telephone operator. They both stayed in those jobs until retirement, well into their 60's.

True to her plan, Emily never let Bill go back to school after Fifth grade. But he had an avid curiosity about the world, reading the Dallas Times Herald, front to back, every day. His strongest wish in life was that his children never have to work as hard for a living as he had done. As you can see, the daughters of Emily and her first husband, Homer Pilgrim, Myrtis and Virgie, grew to be strong willed and independent women. Emily should've been proud of them. The children of Clarence and Emily were also strong, determined people with great capacity to care for their families who followed their own path in the best ways they knew how; with hard work and a 'never give up' attitude.

It might be said that Emily mellowed just a bit as she aged for she did seem to dote on her 22 grandchildren. There are stories of Emily rocking those grandbabies a million miles in a straight backed wooden chair on Vada's front porch; thump clunk thump clunk – back and forth in that rockerless chair.

And other tales of Emily (the grands called her "Mattie") bouncing those babies on her knees while sing-songing the old nursery rhyme:

> *Ride the horsey down to town*
> *To buy some sugar by the pound*
> *On the way, horsey fell down*
> *Dumped my sugar on the ground!*

Of course, the memorable part came when, on the last line, she would straighten her legs and let the grandbaby slide down to her ankles.

When Emily died in her sleep in 1953, Vada discovered Clarence's last letter, the one Rossi brought to her, tucked inside the bodice of her dress. Along with it was her one and only letter to Clarence. Both were faded and wrinkled from time and many refoldings.

Emily's "Come home" letter and Clarence's reply. It simply read

"Leave the lamp on . . ."

About the Author...

Sue Jones McCullough is the granddaughter of Charlie Clarence Jones and only daughter of Bill and Maggie Jones. Sue grew up in DeSoto, a small community in south Dallas County and within spittin' distance of the black land that Emily unsuccessfully tried to farm with Slick and June. Sue was barely a toddler when Emily died so holds no memories of her at all. She grew up hearing tales from her older brothers, Aunt Vada and from her mother, Maggie. Sue contributes her love of words to Bill who was an avid reader regardless of his limited formal education and to her eighth grade English teacher, Lottie Waterman. Married to Andy McCullough since 1982, Sue has no children of her own. Though a dyed in the wool Texan, Sue now lives in Louisville, Kentucky with Andy and an old rescue Shih Tzu named Patricia Margaret, also known as Patty.

Some Good Old Recipes

June's Peach Cobbler

Filling: 8/10 Medium Peaches, peeled and cut into 2 inch chunks
¼ cup Brown Sugar, packed
1 Tablespoon Cornstarch
1 Tablespoon Lemon Juice
½ Teaspoon Vanilla
½ Teaspoon Cinnamon
⅛ Teaspoon Nutmeg
⅛ Teaspoon Salt
Mix all together & pour into 13 by 9 baking dish

Topping: 2 Cups Flour
½ Cup Granulated Sugar
1 ½ Teaspoon Baking Powder
1 ½ Teaspoon Salt
½ Cup Cold Buttermilk
½ Cup Cold Butter, cubed
Whisk all dry ingredients together then spread on
Top of the peach mixture. Place the cubed butter
Around on top of the mix then drizzle with the buttermilk.

Bake at 350 degrees for 40 to 45 minutes until golden and bubbly.

June's Smothered Pork Chops

1 Cup Flour
½ clove Garlic, mashed
1 Medium Onion, diced
½ Teaspoon Cayenne
½ Teaspoon Salt
½ Teaspoon Black Pepper
½ Cup Oil
1 Cup Chicken Broth
½ Cup Buttermilk
4 Bone-In Pork Chops, ½ inch thick

Mix first 6 ingredients together then dredge pork chops in the mixture. With oil in hot skillet, fry chops 3 minutes on each side then remove. Stir 2 Tablespoons of the leftover flour mix into the oil until dissolved. Add the chicken broth and cook down about 5 minutes. Stir in the buttermilk to make gravy. Add the chops back into the skillet. Cover and simmer until the chops are cooked through. Salt and Pepper.

Cook's Chicory Root Coffee

Mince the root into same sized pieces
Roast the pieces; Aroma will tell you when they're done
Grind the pieces; If you don't have a grinder, pound them with a hammer
Brew the ground pieces like any other coffee

It's best to use metal coffee mugs.
The brew is a bit strong and will work right through the glaze on fancy cups.

Cook's Dried Field Beans

2 Cups Oil in Kettle with Lid
4 Onions, any kind will do. Even leaks if that's what you can find or have on hand
3 full Garlic cloves, peeled and mashed
10 pounds Dried Beans – whatever you have on hand

Heat the oil until it sizzles. Toss in onion and garlic. Cook for a couple minutes. Pour in the beans (which you've pre-soaked) and fill the kettle with water. Bring to a boil, lower the heat to simmer with Lid on. Check every hour to make sure beans are still covered with liquid. Cook for about 7 hours.

Serve with cornbread if you have flour, yellow meal, milk and eggs available.

Emily's Collard Greens

2 lbs. collard greens, stemmed and thinly sliced
1 lb. smoked ham hock or salt pork
3 quarts or so water
1 Tablespoon white sugar
salt and pepper to taste pepper sauce for serving

Place collards in large pot and cover with water. Bring to a boil then reduce heat and simmer for 10 minutes. Remove from heat and drain all that water off the greens. Add fresh water, bring back to boil reducing to simmer again for another 10 minutes. Drain again. Add fresh water again. Drain again. Add fresh water again.

About now, when you're ready to open the back door to throw pot and all out into the yard, don't do it!

Now, add the ham, salt pork or bacon grease, sugar and salt & pepper into the pot. Bring back to a boil, reduce heat to simmer, and cook for 30 minutes or until greens are tender, stirring often. Serve with the pepper sauce. Pepper sauce is not the same thing as hot sauce, although that might not be bad, either.

Emily's Corn Bread

1 cup Yellow Cornmeal
2 cups Flour
1 Teaspoon Salt
2 Eggs
2 Cups Buttermilk
¼ Cup Oil
BUTTER – a lot

In a heavy cast iron skillet, heat the oil until it's just about to blaze. While it's heating up, mix all ingredients together. You may not use all the buttermilk. Use just enough to have a loose batter. Pour this batter into the screaming hot skillet. Make sure the children are back and out of the way.

Have the oven preheated to 400 degrees so the skillet doesn't cool off. Bake about 40 minutes until the sides of the cornbread have loosened from the skillet and the top is beginning to brown.

Turn the cornbread out onto a plate, cut into wedges and slather it generously with butter.

Cora's Pound Cake

2 Cups Butter
3 ½ Cups Sugar
12 Eggs
1 Tablespoon Vanilla
1 Teaspoon Salt
3 ½ Cups Flour

Generously grease a Tube pan
Beat Butter until creamy
Add Sugar and blend until fluffy
In a separate bowl, beat eggs, vanilla & salt

Once eggs, vanilla & salt are incorporated, add into butter and sugar mixture. Beat until smooth then scrape down sides and bottom of bowl. Beat on medium-high for 2 minutes.

On low, mix in flour, ¼ cup at a time. When all the flour is mixed in, set on medium and mix until smooth.

Spread evenly into tube pan

Bake on 350 degrees for 60 to 75 minutes. Test with a broom straw. Do not over-bake.

Let cool at least 20 minutes. Run a knife to loosen then invert onto a serving plate.

CPSIA information can be obtained
at www.ICGtesting.com
Printed in the USA
BVHW041505250321
603332BV00010B/1032